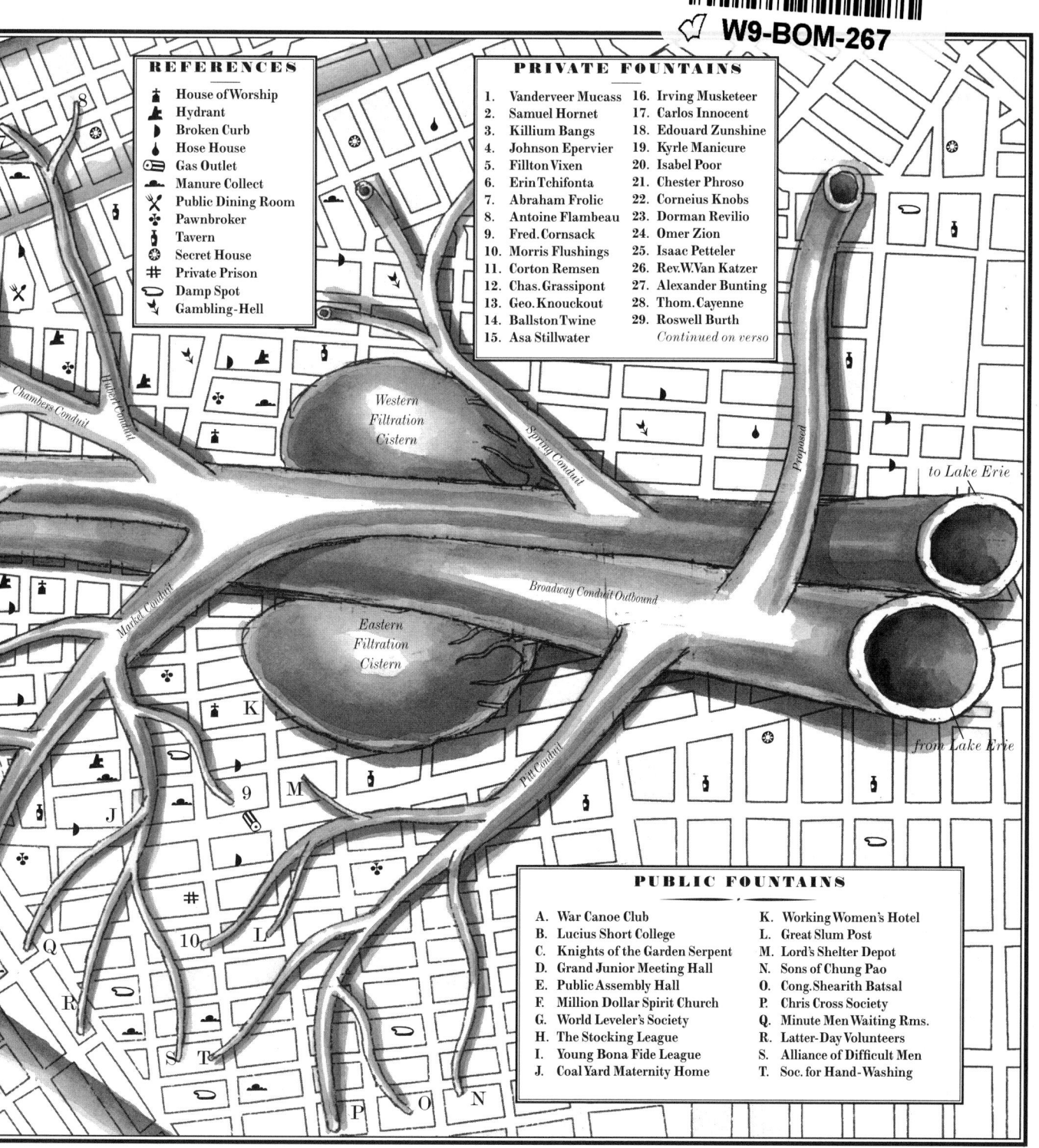

W9-BOM-267

REFERENCES

♁	House of Worship
	Hydrant
◗	Broken Curb
◖	Hose House
⬒	Gas Outlet
⚒	Manure Collect
✕	Public Dining Room
✂	Pawnbroker
♣	Tavern
✵	Secret House
#	Private Prison
⬭	Damp Spot
⚐	Gambling-Hell

PRIVATE FOUNTAINS

1. Vanderveer Mucass
2. Samuel Hornet
3. Killium Bangs
4. Johnson Epervier
5. Fillton Vixen
6. Erin Tchifonta
7. Abraham Frolic
8. Antoine Flambeau
9. Fred. Cornsack
10. Morris Flushings
11. Corton Remsen
12. Chas. Grassipont
13. Geo. Knouckout
14. Ballston Twine
15. Asa Stillwater
16. Irving Musketeer
17. Carlos Innocent
18. Edouard Zunshine
19. Kyrle Manicure
20. Isabel Poor
21. Chester Phroso
22. Corneius Knobs
23. Dorman Revilio
24. Omer Zion
25. Isaac Petteler
26. Rev. W. Van Katzer
27. Alexander Bunting
28. Thom. Cayenne
29. Roswell Burth

Continued on verso

Chambers Conduit

Hamper Conduit

Western Filtration Cistern

Spring Conduit

Proposed

to Lake Erie

Market Conduit

Eastern Filtration Cistern

Broadway Conduit Outbound

from Lake Erie

Pitt Conduit

PUBLIC FOUNTAINS

A. War Canoe Club
B. Lucius Short College
C. Knights of the Garden Serpent
D. Grand Junior Meeting Hall
E. Public Assembly Hall
F. Million Dollar Spirit Church
G. World Leveler's Society
H. The Stocking League
I. Young Bona Fide League
J. Coal Yard Maternity Home
K. Working Women's Hotel
L. Great Slum Post
M. Lord's Shelter Depot
N. Sons of Chung Pao
O. Cong. Shearith Batsal
P. Chris Cross Society
Q. Minute Men Waiting Rms.
R. Latter-Day Volunteers
S. Alliance of Difficult Men
T. Soc. for Hand-Washing

THE
JEW
OF
NEW YORK
——

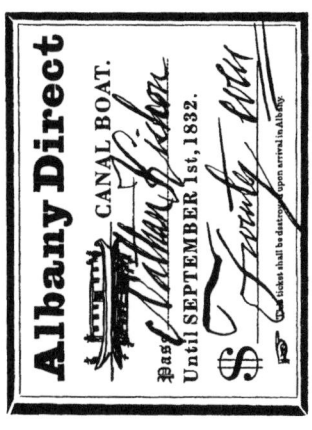

Albany Direct

CANAL BOAT.

Until SEPTEMBER 1st, 1832.

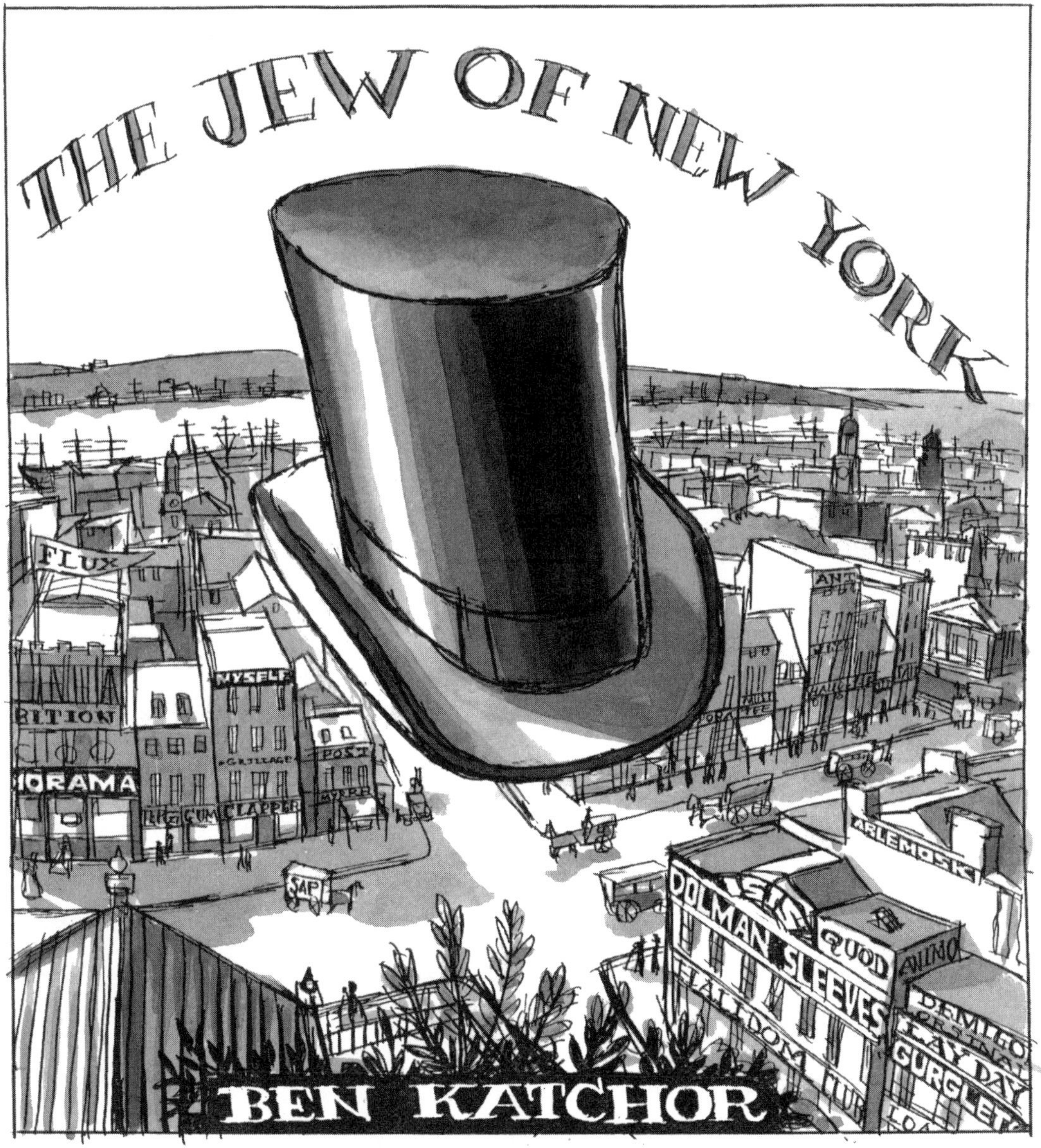
THE JEW OF NEW YORK
FLUX
MYSELF
POST
CLAPPER
SAP
DOLMAN SLEEVES
QUOD
BEN KATCHOR

PANTHEON BOOKS
New York

PUBLIC CITATIONS

Page 3, panel 5: Francisco Lopez de Gómara's *Historia de las Indias*, 1553.
Page 6, panel 8: M. M. Noah, *The National Advocate*, 1821.
Page 7: *The Ten Tribes of Israel Historically Identified with the Aborigines of the Western Hemisphere*, by Mrs. Simon, 1836.
Page 8: Ibid.
Page 11, panel 6: M.M. Noah, "Proclamation to the Jews," Sept. 15, 1825.
Page 19, panel 6: Berakhot, 9:1.
Page 23, panel 8: M. Valtinau, *Jerusalem in the New World*, 1828.
Page 24, panel 6: Dr. C. Leannox, *Communing with the Brutes*, 1829.
Page 27, panel 5: Joseph Priestly, *Experiments and Observations on Different Kinds of Air*, 1790.
Page 28, panel 3: Ibid.
Page 32: Abraham Abulafia, *The Book of Eternal Life*, 1280.
Page 36, panel 4: Rabbi J. Ollveys, "On Public Nakedness," 1927.
Page 36, panel 6: Anonymous, Unpublished Sermon, 1830.
Page 43, panel 9: *Niles' Register*, Nov. 28, 1829.
Page 47: Châteaubriand, *L'Intinéraire de Paris à Jérusalem et de Jérusalem à Paris*, 1811.
Page 72, panel 4: Deuteronomy, 4:25.
Page 89, panel 8: Christopher Marlowe, Machiavel from *The Jew of Malta*, 1633.
Page 92, panel 8: *The Evening Star*, Oct. 5, 1833.

LIBRARY OF CONGRESS
CATALOGING-IN-PUBLICATION DATA

Katchor, Ben.
The Jew of New York : a historical romance / Ben Katchor.
p.   cm.   ISBN 0-375-70097-8   I. Title.   PN6727.K28J48   1999
741.5'973—dc21   98-23996   CIP

www.pantheonbooks.com

Designed by Ben Katchor and Misha Beletsky

Printed in the United States of America
First Paperback Edition
9 8 7 6 5 4 3 2 1

Nathan Kishon

Mr. Marah

Prof. Solidus

Isaac Azarael with stick

Yosl Feinbroyt

Francis Oriole

Enoch Letushim

Man in an India Rubber Suit

ON A TEPID AUGUST AFTERNOON IN THE YEAR 1830, MESSRS. PEPSIN & SHADRACH, THE CURRENT MANAGERS OF "THE NEW WORLD THEATER," MEET WITH THEIR ARTISTIC EMPLOYEES TO FINALIZE THE COMING SEASON'S REPERTORY.

THE CHOICE OF AN "INDIAN" PLAY IS LEFT TO THE SCENIC DECORATOR, MR. SAMSON GERGEL.

"A CHILD OF NATURE" OR "TUSCATOMBA"?

THE SEASON'S SHAKE-SPEAREAN PLAY IS A FAVORITE OF THE DISTINGUISHED TRAGIC ACTRESS, MRS. JELMOTH.

"MACBETH"

THE "PATRIOTIC" PLAY WILL BE ONE WRITTEN BY THEIR MUSICAL DIRECTOR, MR. PRUINOSE.

"OVER THE FALLS AND BACK AGAIN"

AS FOR THE SEASON'S COMEDY, THERE IS NO DISCUSSION. COPIES OF A NEW PLAY, "THE JEW OF NEW YORK," ARE HANDED OUT.

MR. GERGEL, THE COMPANY'S ONE JEW, IS ALL TOO FAMILIAR WITH THESE "HEBRAIC" COMEDIES.

IT WAS HE WHO DESIGNED THE UPROARIOUS "MESSIAH'S ARRIVAL" SCENE IN THE LONG-RUNNING SUCCESS "OUR FIRST-FLOOR JEW."

AND SO, FOR THE REMAIN-ING DAYS OF THAT LONG SUMMER, HE STUDIES THE SCRIPT WITH AN EYE TOWARD BRINGING OUT THOSE EFFECTS WHICH WOULD MOST EXCITE AN AUDIENCE.

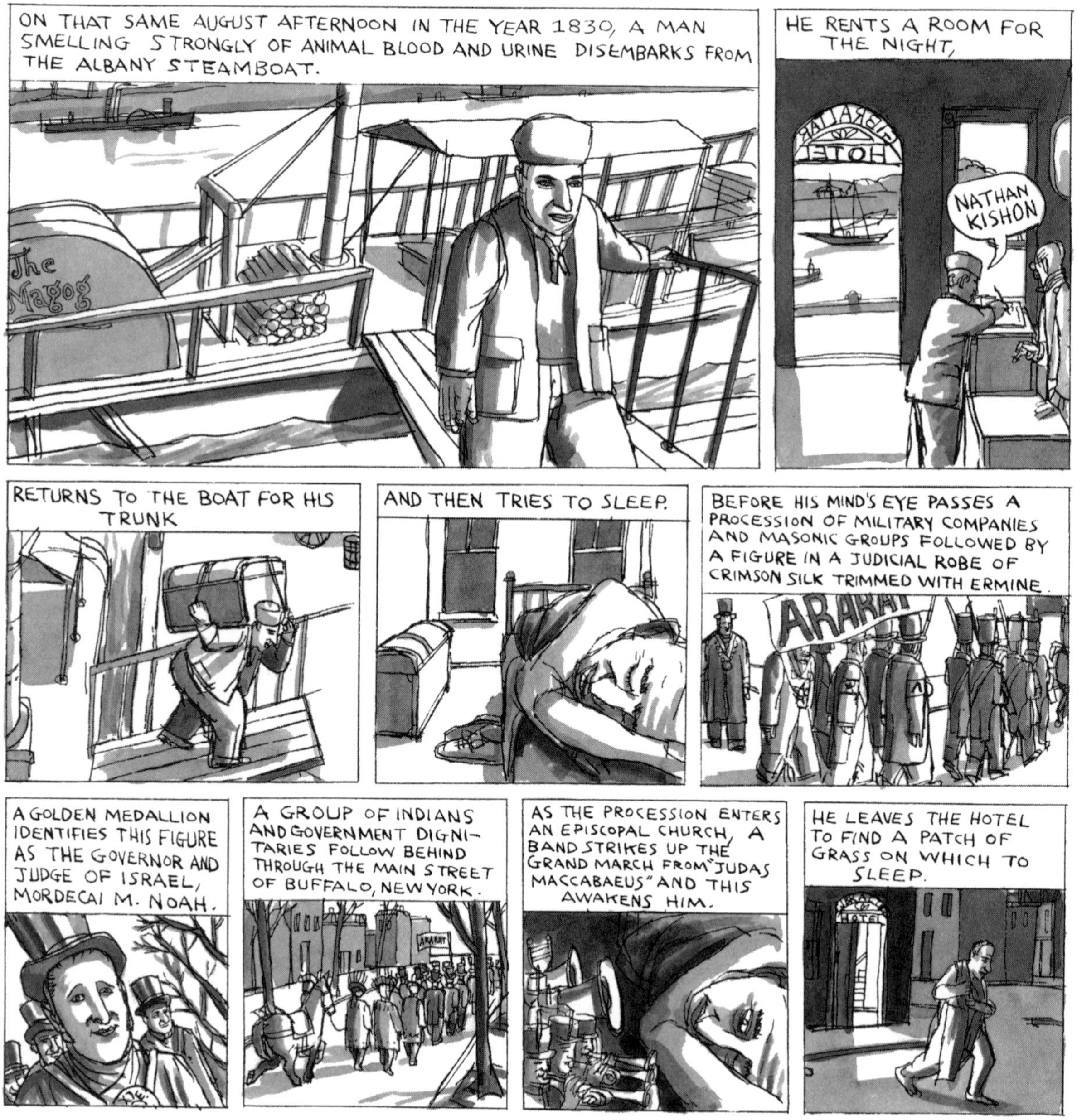

ON THAT SAME AUGUST AFTERNOON IN THE YEAR 1830, A MAN SMELLING STRONGLY OF ANIMAL BLOOD AND URINE DISEMBARKS FROM THE ALBANY STEAMBOAT.
The Magog
HE RENTS A ROOM FOR THE NIGHT,
GIBRALTAR HOTEL
NATHAN KISHON
RETURNS TO THE BOAT FOR HIS TRUNK
AND THEN TRIES TO SLEEP.
BEFORE HIS MIND'S EYE PASSES A PROCESSION OF MILITARY COMPANIES AND MASONIC GROUPS FOLLOWED BY A FIGURE IN A JUDICIAL ROBE OF CRIMSON SILK TRIMMED WITH ERMINE.
ARARAT
A GOLDEN MEDALLION IDENTIFIES THIS FIGURE AS THE GOVERNOR AND JUDGE OF ISRAEL, MORDECAI M. NOAH.
A GROUP OF INDIANS AND GOVERNMENT DIGNITARIES FOLLOW BEHIND THROUGH THE MAIN STREET OF BUFFALO, NEW YORK.
AS THE PROCESSION ENTERS AN EPISCOPAL CHURCH, A BAND STRIKES UP THE GRAND MARCH FROM "JUDAS MACCABAEUS" AND THIS AWAKENS HIM.
HE LEAVES THE HOTEL TO FIND A PATCH OF GRASS ON WHICH TO SLEEP.
HOTEL

AFTER AN EVENING MEETING OF THE SHEARITH BATSAL BURIAL SOCIETY...

ISAAC AZARAEL, A MIDDLEMAN IN THE ORIENTAL BUTTON TRADE, WANDERS TOWARD THE NORTH RIVER DOCKS TO SEE IF A CERTAIN SHIP HAS ARRIVED.

THREE HUNDRED POUNDS OF MOTHER-OF-PEARL AT FOUR CENTS A POUND...

ON A SMALL PLOT OF GRASS IN FRONT OF THE GIBRALTAR HOTEL, HE SEES A SLEEPING FIGURE WRAPPED IN A BLANKET.

A NAKED INDIAN!

HE RECALLS A FRAGMENT OF A LECTURE HE ONCE HEARD

The Ten Lost Tribes of Israel HISTORICALLY IDENTIFIED with the ABORIGINES of The Western Hemisphere. Mr. ___ Simon

THEY ARE ALL VERY LIKE JEWS, IN APPEARANCE AND VOICE, FOR THEY HAVE LARGE NOSES AND SPEAK THROUGH THE THROAT...

HE STUDIES THE FACE AND SEES A FAMILIAR CONFIGURATION OF FEATURES.

THE POOR MAN...WITHOUT A BED OR CLOTHING...

A CLIPPER SHIP GLIDES SILENTLY UPSTREAM

AND MR. AZARAEL RUNS TO CATCH A GLIMPSE OF THE NAME PAINTED ON ITS BOW.

MAYBE THE "PALAMABRON."

SAMSON GERGEL, SCENIC DECORATOR OF "THE NEW WORLD THEATER," CONCLUDES HIS FIRST READING OF THE SEASON'S NEW COMEDY...

"THE JEW OF NEW YORK"! IT'S NOTHING MORE THAN A THINLY VEILED BURLESQUE OF THE LIFE, TO DATE, OF MAJOR MORDECAI NOAH.

THE ACTOR, DAIZY, WILL TRANSFORM HIMSELF INTO A CARICATURE OF THIS EMINENT CITIZEN — A "MAJOR HAM" WITH A "GHETTO STOOP" VISIBLE FROM THE HIGHEST BALCONY. FOR HIS PATRIOTIC DEVOTION THE PROTAGONIST IS ACCUSED OF OPPORTUNISM...

FOR HIS GENEROSITY OF SPIRIT HE IS DECRIED AS A VOLUPTUARY. THE MANAGEMENT HAS ADVERTISED ALL NEW SCENERY — A NAVAL BATTLE, A TUNISIAN PANORAMA, ETC.

I CAN ONLY ENDEAVOR TO AWAKEN THE AUDIENCE TO SOME DEEPER TRUTH THROUGH MY SCENIC DECOR. THE REST IS A MATTER FOR THE COURTS TO PURSUE.

FOR THREE THOUSAND DOLLARS WORTH OF LATHE AND STAFF PLASTER, MAJ. NOAH'S ENEMIES WILL HAVE AN ENTERTAINING EVENING AT THE THEATER.

GERGEL RETURNS TO HIS DIVAN AND PROCEEDS TO ENVISION A CURTAIN RISING TO REVEAL THE STAGE AS SET FOR ACT 1, SCENE 1...
A STREET IN PHILADELPHIA, C.1789.

WHERE, AS A CHILD OF THREE, MAJ. HAM CLAIMS TO HAVE SEEN THE AGED BENJAMIN FRANKLIN BEING TAKEN FOR A WALK.

FOR ACT 2, SCENE 2, GERGEL RECONSTRUCTS THE CHESTNUT STREET THEATER IN PHILADELPHIA, C.1800, WHERE, AS A BOY, MAJ. HAM BEGAN HIS LIFELONG FRIENDSHIP WITH THE DRAMA.

LIKE OTHERS IN HIS PROFESSION, THE ACTOR MAYNARD DAIZY MANAGES TO STAND OUT IN A CROWD BY WEARING AN OVERSIZED HAT AND A FROCK COAT OF A RARE, PALE GREEN COLOR.

WHEN NOT ON THE STAGE, HE SPENDS HIS TIME AT VARIOUS PUBLIC DINING ROOMS

MAKING UP FOR THE MEALS I MISSED AS A YOUNG MAN

BETWEEN SPOONFULS OF TURTLE SOUP, HE GIVES SOME THOUGHT TO HIS NEXT LEADING ROLE — THAT OF MAJ. HAM IN THE NEW COMEDY, "THE JEW OF NEW YORK."

THERE WAS GARDINER'S SHYLOCK IN PHILADELPHIA...

A MOTH-EATEN EXOTIC RIGHT OUT OF THE OLD TESTAMENT

AND THEN THERE WAS MORRAY'S FLACID LITTLE OPERATOR IN "OUR FIRST-FLOOR JEW" AT THE OLYMPIA

IN FACT, DAIZY HAD ONLY KNOWN TWO JEWS IN THE FLESH...

TURTLE SOUP

THAT PEDDLER IN ALBANY... A HUMAN PACK ANIMAL

AND SAMSON GERGEL, THE SCENIC DECORATOR

THE SOUP HERE IS QUITE PIQUANT.

FRESH TURTLE SOUP

THANK YOU, BUT I'VE ALREADY...

A SINGLE, THREE-POUND TONGUE PROVIDED ALL THE EVIDENCE NECESSARY TO FIND NATHAN KISHON GUILTY OF "WILLFUL DECEPTION AND CARELESS PERFORMANCE OF A RITUAL DUTY."

WAS THAT FIVE YEARS AGO?

HE HAD BEEN HIRED BY A BUTCHER NAMED SPITZ TO PREPARE A CERTAIN NUMBER OF ANIMALS FOR THE JEWS' MARKET.

IN ADDITION TO HIS SALARY, KISHON WAS GIVEN THE TONGUES OF THOSE ANIMALS WHICH HE HAD SLAUGHTERED.

MOST OF THESE ORGANS HE IMMEDIATELY SOLD TO SUPPLEMENT HIS INCOME.

THE DIFFERENCE IN COLOR AND CONSISTENCY BETWEEN A KOSHER AND NON-KOSHER TONGUE IS PLAIN TO SEE.

WHERE DID YOU BUY THIS?

BUT AS JEWISH LEARNING WAS AT A LOW POINT IN THE CITY AT THAT TIME,

ARE YOU KISHON THE SHOYKHET?

THE TONGUES WERE INDISCRIMINATELY TOSSED INTO THE SAME BARREL UNTIL IT WAS FULL.

IT WAS A MISCHIEVOUS DELIVERY BOY ... A CHILD'S HARMLESS PRANK ...

HOWEVER, "AN ISRAELITE WHO HAS SINNED RITUALLY IS STILL AN ISRAELITE."

THEY INTEND TO ROB ME OF MY LIVELIHOOD.

"I AM TIRED OF SEEING A NATION OF SEVEN MILLIONS OF PEOPLE, RICH AND INTELLIGENT, WANDERING ABOUT THE WORLD WITHOUT A HOME WHICH THEY CAN CLAIM AS THEIR OWN AND LOOKING TO THE RESTORATION TO AN ANCIENT COUNTY, WHICH ONE-EIGHTH WOULD NOT INHABIT, IF THEY RE-COVERED IT TOMORROW..."

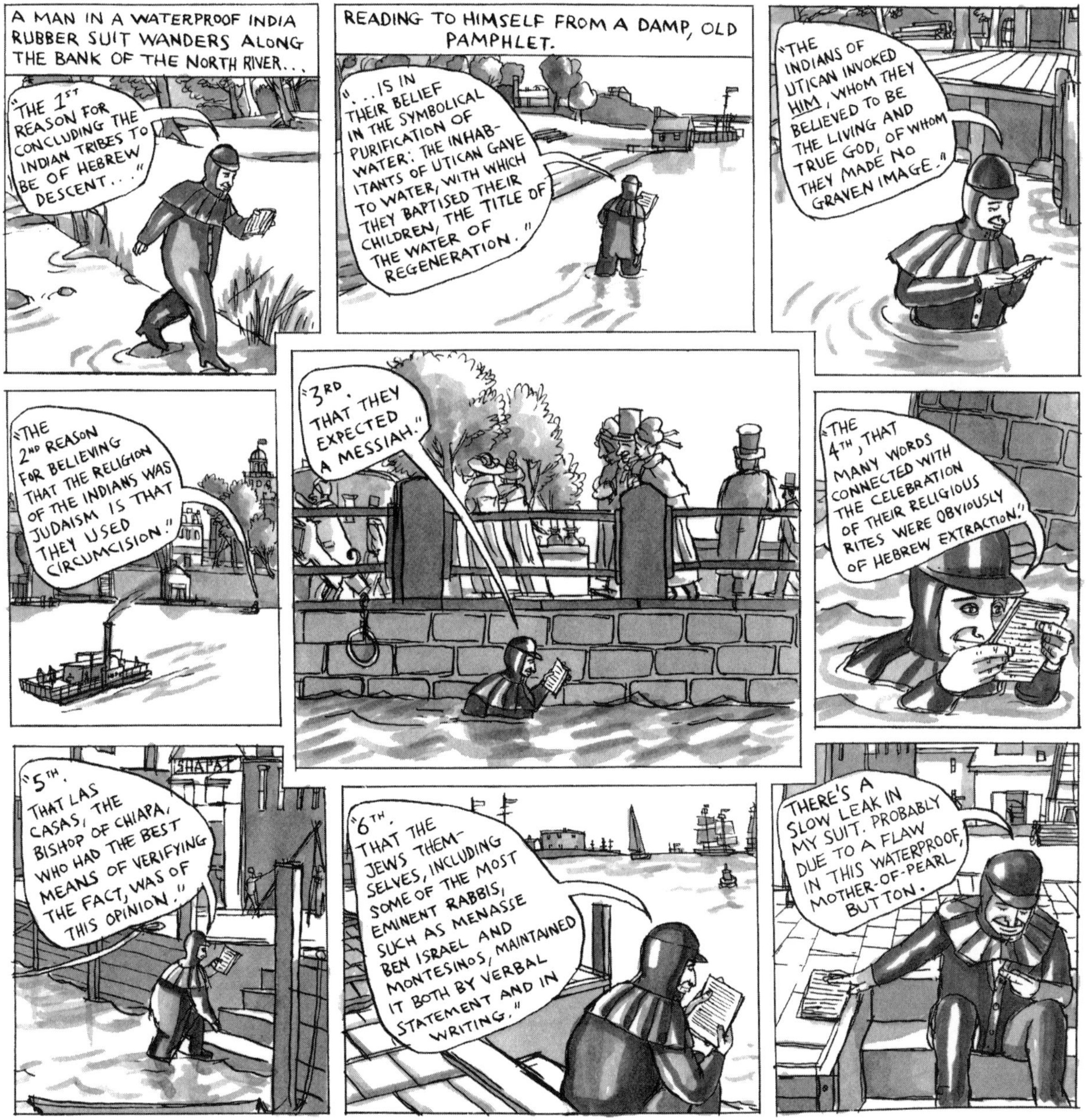
A MAN IN A WATERPROOF INDIA RUBBER SUIT WANDERS ALONG THE BANK OF THE NORTH RIVER...
"THE 1ST REASON FOR CONCLUDING THE INDIAN TRIBES TO BE OF HEBREW DESCENT..."
READING TO HIMSELF FROM A DAMP, OLD PAMPHLET.
"...IS IN THEIR BELIEF IN THE SYMBOLICAL PURIFICATION OF WATER; THE INHABITANTS OF UTICAN GAVE TO WATER, WITH WHICH THEY BAPTISED THEIR CHILDREN, THE TITLE OF THE WATER OF REGENERATION."
"THE INDIANS OF UTICAN INVOKED HIM, WHOM THEY BELIEVED TO BE THE LIVING AND TRUE GOD, OF WHOM THEY MADE NO GRAVEN IMAGE."
"THE 2ND REASON FOR BELIEVING THAT THE RELIGION OF THE INDIANS WAS JUDAISM IS THAT THEY USED CIRCUMCISION."
"3RD. THAT THEY EXPECTED A MESSIAH."
"THE 4TH, THAT MANY WORDS CONNECTED WITH THE CELEBRATION OF THEIR RELIGIOUS RITES WERE OBVIOUSLY OF HEBREW EXTRACTION."
"5TH. THAT LAS CASAS, THE BISHOP OF CHIAPA, WHO HAD THE BEST MEANS OF VERIFYING THE FACT, WAS OF THIS OPINION."
SHAPAT
"6TH. THAT THE JEWS THEMSELVES, INCLUDING SOME OF THE MOST EMINENT RABBIS, SUCH AS MENASSE BEN ISRAEL AND MONTESINOS, MAINTAINED IT BOTH BY VERBAL STATEMENT AND IN WRITING."
THERE'S A SLOW LEAK IN MY SUIT. PROBABLY DUE TO A FLAW IN THIS WATERPROOF, MOTHER-OF-PEARL BUTTON.

ISAAC AZARAEL, A MIDDLEMAN IN THE ORIENTAL BUTTON TRADE, WAITS IMPATIENTLY FOR "THE PALAMABRON" TO ARRIVE.

TWO DAYS LATE

HE NOTICES A MAN WEARING A FULL SET OF MOTHER-OF-PEARL BUTTONS.

I FEAR THE WORST

"THE 7TH IS THE RESEMBLANCE WHICH MANY CEREMONIES AND RITES OF THE INDIANS BEAR TO THOSE OF THE JEWS."

"THE 8TH IS THE SIMILITUDE WHICH EXISTED BETWEEN THE INDIAN AND HEBREW MORAL LAWS."

A TOTAL LOSS.

"THE 9TH IS THE KNOWLEDGE WHICH THE MEXICAN AND PERUVIAN TRADITIONS SUPPLIED, THAT THE INDIANS POSSESSED THE HISTORY CONTAINED IN THE PENTATEUCH."

"10TH. THE TRACES OF JEWISH HISTORY, TRADITIONS, LAWS, CUSTOMS, MANNERS, WHICH ARE FOUND IN THE MEXICAN PAINTINGS."

ON THE OTHER SIDE OF THE RIVER,

"11TH. THE FREQUENCY OF SACRIFICE AMONGST THE INDIANS, AND THE RELIGIOUS CONSECRATION OF THE BLOOD AND FAT OF THE VICTIMS."

IN A RUDE TAVERN,

"12TH. THE STYLE OF THE ARCHITECTURE OF THEIR TEMPLES."

AN INDIAN DRINKS A GLASS OF WHISKY.

"AND 13TH. THE FRINGES WHICH THE INDIANS WEAR FASTENED TO THEIR GARMENTS."

THE TEN TRIBES OF ISRAEL

HISTORICALLY IDENTIFIED

WITH THE

ABORIGINES

OF THE

WESTERN HEMISPHERE

By Mrs. Simon

. . . .

"Behold! I was left alone: — these, where had they been?—"
Isaiah XLIX. 21.

. . . .

PUBLISHED BY
THE SOCIETY FOR THE REDEMPTION
OF ISRAELITIC PEOPLES
CORNER STREET, LONDON
1830

ON A PATCH OF GRASS ACROSS FROM THE GIBRALTAR HOTEL, NATHAN KISHON AWAKENS FROM A LICENTIOUS DREAM.

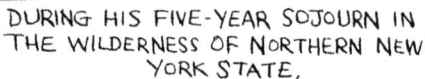

DURING HIS FIVE-YEAR SOJOURN IN THE WILDERNESS OF NORTHERN NEW YORK STATE,

FEWER PIGS ARE FORAGING ON BROADWAY.

THE CITY SEEMS TO HAVE UNDERGONE A WONDROUS TRANSFORMATION.

THIS THEATER, BURNT TO THE GROUND, HAS BEEN REBUILT.

THERE IS A NEW MYSTERY TO WOMEN'S CLOTHING.

AND THE JEWS' BURIAL GROUND IS NOW A SIZEABLE NECROPOLIS.

ירדת
PIEXO
1810

HIRAM

AN OLD ACQUAINTANCE IS STARTLED BY THE SIGHT OF NATHAN KISHON.

BAREFOOT AND IN RAGS!

CAN IT BE THE SAME MAN?

CHEMIST

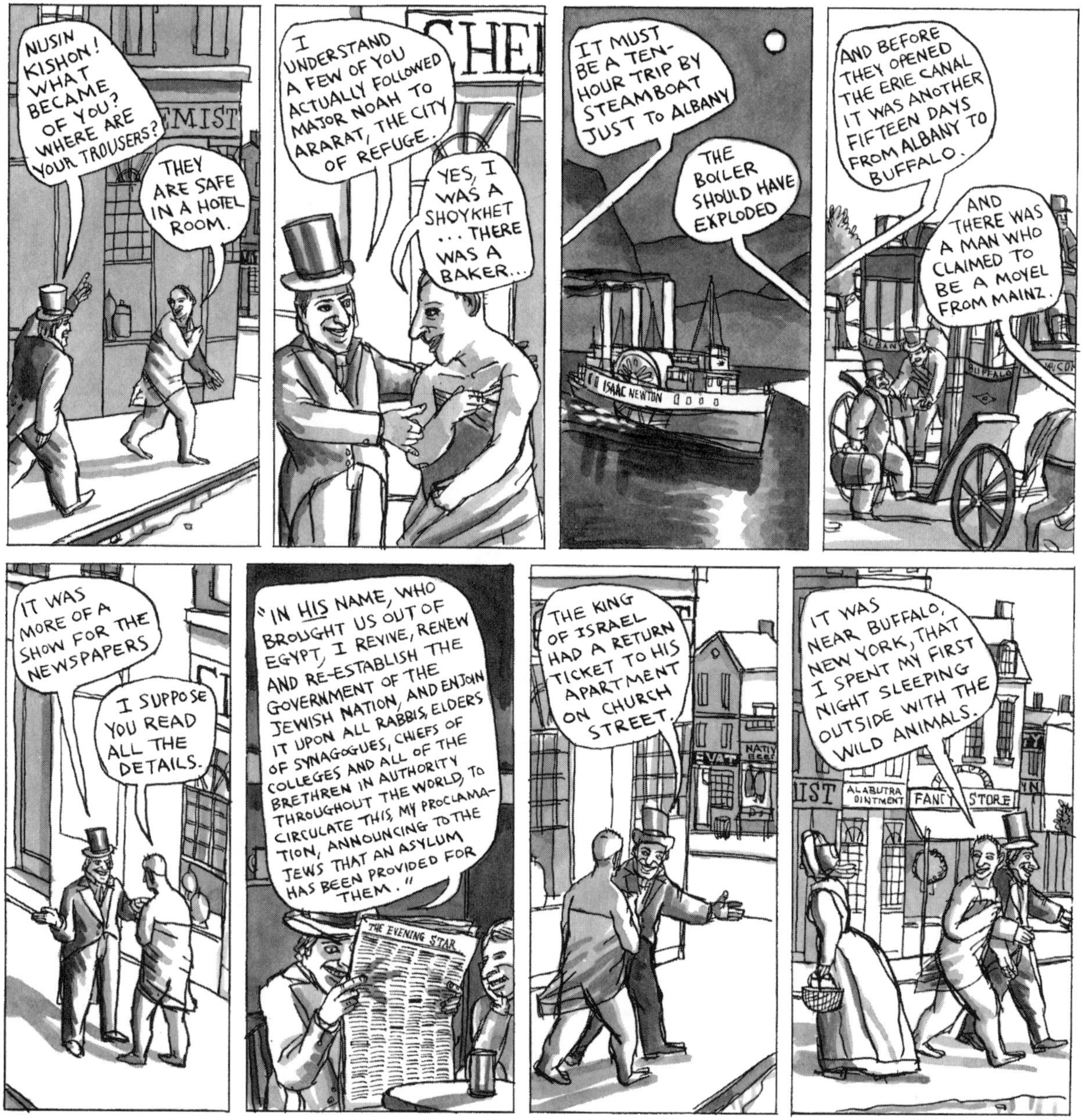
NUSIN KISHON! WHAT BECAME OF YOU? WHERE ARE YOUR TROUSERS?
THEY ARE SAFE IN A HOTEL ROOM.
I UNDERSTAND A FEW OF YOU ACTUALLY FOLLOWED MAJOR NOAH TO ARARAT, THE CITY OF REFUGE.
YES, I WAS A SHOYKHET . . . THERE WAS A BAKER...
IT MUST BE A TEN-HOUR TRIP BY STEAMBOAT JUST TO ALBANY
THE BOILER SHOULD HAVE EXPLODED
ISAAC NEWTON
AND BEFORE THEY OPENED THE ERIE CANAL IT WAS ANOTHER FIFTEEN DAYS FROM ALBANY TO BUFFALO.
AND THERE WAS A MAN WHO CLAIMED TO BE A MOYEL FROM MAINZ.
IT WAS MORE OF A SHOW FOR THE NEWSPAPERS
I SUPPOSE YOU READ ALL THE DETAILS.
"IN HIS NAME, WHO BROUGHT US OUT OF EGYPT, I REVIVE, RENEW AND RE-ESTABLISH THE GOVERNMENT OF THE JEWISH NATION, AND ENJOIN IT UPON ALL RABBIS, ELDERS OF SYNAGOGUES, CHIEFS OF COLLEGES AND ALL OF THE BRETHREN IN AUTHORITY THROUGHOUT THE WORLD, TO CIRCULATE THIS, MY PROCLAMATION, ANNOUNCING TO THE JEWS THAT AN ASYLUM HAS BEEN PROVIDED FOR THEM."
THE EVENING STAR
THE KING OF ISRAEL HAD A RETURN TICKET TO HIS APARTMENT ON CHURCH STREET.
IT WAS NEAR BUFFALO, NEW YORK, THAT I SPENT MY FIRST NIGHT SLEEPING OUTSIDE WITH THE WILD ANIMALS.
ALABUTRA OINTMENT
FANCY STORE

COME IN HERE OFF THE STREET. HAVE SOMETHING TO DRINK.

CHALDEAN GARDENS

IT WAS ON THAT DAY, SEPTEMBER 15th 1825. THE PEOPLE OF BUFFALO WERE CURIOUS TO SEE THIS PROCESSION OF JEWS AND THEIR SUPPORTERS MARCHING TOWARD GRAND ISLAND.

WERE THESE THE CHOSEN PEOPLE THEY HAD READ ABOUT IN THE BIBLE?

ARARAT

WORD HAD ALREADY SPREAD THROUGH THE TOWN THAT THIS REFUGE FOR THE DOWNTRODDEN JEWS OF THE EARTH WAS NOTHING MORE THAN A LAND SPECULATION SCHEME.

Lake Ontario

Niagara Falls

Chippawa

GRAND ISLAND

Niagara River

Buffalo

Lake Erie

A MAN IN THE CROWD ASKED ME A SERIES OF INSULTING QUESTIONS.

HOW WILL THE JEWS ADAPT TO AN AGRICULTURAL LIFE? AND WHAT BECOMES OF THEIR AMERICAN CITIZENSHIP?

Khatan New York

HE HAD ONLY A VAGUE UNDERSTANDING OF THE HISTORICAL SIGNIFICANCE OF THE EVENT.

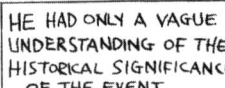

YOU SEE, THIS IS ONLY A TEMPORARY ASYLUM. ULTIMATELY WE WILL RECOVER PALESTINE.

THIS MAN, I LATER DISCOVERED, HAD AMASSED A SMALL FORTUNE BY LEASING EQUIPMENT TO LOCAL TRAPPERS AND INVESTING THE PROCEEDS IN BEAVER PELTS.

GA-NĂ-DIKE-HO E-YOSE.

WE-YO'

I BELIEVE THAT HE WAS A BAPTISED JEW WHO HAD LIVED FOR SO MANY YEARS IN THE WILD THAT HE NO LONGER MAINTAINED ANY RELIGIOUS AFFILIATIONS.

WOULD YOU CARE FOR SOME OYSTERS ON THE HALF-SHELL?

AS IT TURNED OUT, THERE WEREN'T ENOUGH BOATS TO FERRY THE CROWD TO GRAND ISLAND...

WAITER! WAITER!

AND SO THE CORNERSTONE-LAYING CEREMONIES WERE HELD IN THE EPISCOPAL CHURCH OF BUFFALO.

UNDER THE PROTECTION OF THE GREAT AMERICAN UNION THIS STATE COULD EQUAL PALESTINE IN SIZE, BUT WOULD HAVE MANY ADVANTAGES.

THE CROWD WAS ASSURED THAT THE CORNERSTONE WOULD BE SET INTO A MONUMENT OF BRICK AND WOOD WHICH HAD BEEN ERECTED ON THE ISLAND.

שמע ישראל י״י אלהינו י״י אחד

ARARAT

A CITY OF REFUGE FOR THE JEWS
FOUNDED BY MORDECAI NOAH, IN THE MONTH OF TIZRI 5586 SEPT. 1825 & IN THE 50TH YEAR OF AMERICAN INDEPENDENCE

NO PROVISIONS HAD BEEN MADE THAT EVENING FOR THE NEW SETTLERS.

CAN YOU RECOMMEND A BOARDING HOUSE... A KOSHER DINING ROOM?

?

THE FUR TRADER SAW THAT I WAS LOST AND INVITED ME TO SPEND THE NIGHT.

I HAVE PLENTY OF SPARE ROOM.

I FOLLOWED HIM THROUGH THE WOODS FOR AN HOUR OR MORE.

HE MUST LIVE ON THE OUTSKIRTS OF BUFFALO.

WHEN IT BECAME DARK, HE STOPPED AND MADE HIMSELF COMFORTABLE AGAINST A TREE.

AND SO I CAME TO SPEND MY FIRST NIGHT SLEEPING OUTSIDE WITH THE WILD ANIMALS.

DO YOU KNOW WHAT'S PLAYING THIS SEASON AT THE BOWERY THEATER?

UNSOLD AND DISCARDED NEW YORK CITY NEWSPAPERS SOMEHOW FIND THEIR WAY INTO THE OUTDOOR PRIVIES OF EVEN THE SMALLEST UPSTATE VILLAGES.

ZHALOUP.

HE CHOSE TO READ THE THEATER NOTICES AND THUS ACQUIRED A THOROUGH KNOWLEDGE OF THE NAMES AND PHYSICAL ATTRIBUTES OF THE CURRENT STAGE ACTRESSES.

AN INCIPIENT JEALOUSY HAD PROMPTED HIM TO STOP IN BUFFALO THAT DAY FOR A GLIMPSE OF MORDECAI NOAH — THE LUCKY MAN WHOSE NAME WAS NOW LINKED FOREVER WITH THAT OF THE FAMOUS ENGLISH ACTRESS MISS PATELLA.

HE WROTE "SHE WOULD BE A SOLDIER" ESPECIALLY FOR HER.

CURIOUSLY, HE HAD NO INTEREST IN ATTENDING ACTUAL THEATRICAL PERFORMANCES.

I UNDERSTAND THE PENIEL COMPANY IS PLAYING IN BUFFALO.

WHO NEEDS TO SIT TWO HOURS IN A HOT, CROWDED ROOM.

MISS PATELLA

1825
World Tour
1831

THIS TALK OF FAMILIAR THINGS TRANSFORMED THE FOREST INTO A COMFORTABLE PARLOR OF BARK AND ROTTED LEAVES — AND I SOON FELL ASLEEP.

THIS IS MISS PATELLA AS A FEMALE ZOUAVE.

IN THE MORNING, HE PREPARED A BREAKFAST OF THINLY SLICED, CURED MEAT ON BLACK BREAD.

BEAVER'S TAIL.

ZHALOUP.

IT WAS MY INTENTION TO RETURN TO THE VICINITY OF GRAND ISLAND, AND, BEFORE THE ARRIVAL OF A MULTITUDE OF EUROPEAN COMPETITORS, ESTABLISH MYSELF AS A SHOYKHET IN THE NEW, JEWISH STATE OF ARARAT.

BUT MY HOST HAD HEARD FROM A PASSING INDIAN, WHILE I SLEPT, THAT NOAH AND HIS ENTOURAGE WERE ALREADY ON THEIR WAY BACK TO NEW YORK CITY.

SÄ-WEN-NIS'-HÄT?

GÄ-NO'-NO.

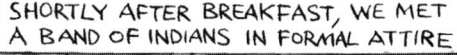
SHORTLY AFTER BREAKFAST, WE MET A BAND OF INDIANS IN FORMAL ATTIRE.

THEY SAY MAJOR NOAH HAS LEFT IN SHAME.

THEY CAME TO GIVE THANKS TO THE WATERS SURROUNDING GRAND ISLAND.

ALTHOUGH THEY WISH TO ENFOLD THE ENTIRE INDIAN RACE INTO ONE FAMILY, THE HODENOSAUNEE NATION CANNOT BE SUBSUMED BY MAJOR NOAH'S TRIBE OF JEWS.

WHAT PROOF HAS BEEN OFFERED OF THEIR DESCENT FROM A COMMON MOTHER? THEY, UNDERSTANDABLY, SUSPECT TRICKERY AND DECEIT.

IT WAS IN ALL THE NEWSPAPERS. EVEN HIS CLOSE FRIENDS HESITATED TO PURCHASE LOTS ON GRAND ISLAND. THE JEWS OF THE WORLD, EXCEPT FOR A FEW, IGNORED NOAH'S CALL.

THE MEMBERS OF THE LOST TRIBES, THE KARAITES, THE SAMARITANS PREFERRED TO REMAIN LOST... WHERE IS THAT WAITER?

MY HOST SAW MAJOR NOAH'S DEFEAT AS A PERSONAL VICTORY.

WHAT WILL MISS PATELLA THINK OF THIS "ARARAT" PLAY? IT HAS NO THIRD ACT!

IN A MAGNANIMOUS GESTURE, HE TOOK ME UNDER HIS WING AS A FELLOW, LOST JEW.

I WAS BORN MOISHE KETZELBOURD BUT THE INDIANS CALL ME MAURICE COUGAR.

HE AFFECTED THE DRESS AND MANNERS OF A WOODSMAN, BUT WAS, IN FACT, NO MORE THAN AN OPEN-AIR ACCOUNTANT.

"604 BEAVER PELTS, 407 MUSKRAT PELTS AND 34 OUNCES OF CASTOREUM."

CASTOREUM?

IT WAS GOOD FOR BUSINESS, HE SAID, THAT I CARRIED A SET OF FINE ENGLISH KNIVES AND WAS ABLE TO HOLD FORTH UPON THE FINE POINTS OF BUTCHERY.

IT'S TO BE DONE AS PAINLESSLY AS POSSIBLE.

I SOON LEARNED MORE OF HIS PAST LIFE: OF HIS WHITEWASHED VILLA ON THE SHORE OF LAKE CAYUGA AND OF HIS WIFE AND THREE DAUGHTERS.

RAMONA IS A LAPSED ANABAPTIST, BUT I SAW TO IT THAT OUR GIRLS WERE CHRISTENED INTO THE CHURCH OF THE FULL IMMERSION.

AT FIRST, HIS SALES EXPEDITIONS WERE ARRANGED SO AS TO ALLOW HIM TO RETURN HOME EACH WEEK FOR SUNDAY DINNER.

THIS NECKTIE, IT BINDS ME.

OVER THE YEARS, AS HIS BUSINESS TOOK HIM FARTHER AFIELD, HIS VISITS HOME BECAME INCREASINGLY RARE.

I PRAY THAT THE ENCLOSED BANK DRAFT WILL TIDE YOU OVER UNTIL NEW YEAR'S DAY WHEN I HOPE TO FIND MYSELF, AGAIN, AT YOUR SIDE.

IN HIS BEGRIMED EYES, THIS WAS A FINE DOMESTIC ARRANGEMENT.

WITH THE OPENING OF THE ERIE CANAL, I AM NEVER MORE THAN FOURTEEN DAYS FROM HOME.

OTHER THAN FOR THE OCCASIONAL PURCHASE OF A CHEAP THEATRICAL PRINT, HE HAD NO USE FOR MONEY. HIS DEALINGS IN THE FUR TRADE WERE AN END UNTO THEMSELVES.

THE BEAVER IS THE ONLY CREATURE, BESIDES MAN, TO ALTER NATURE ON A GRAND SCALE FOR ITS OWN BENEFIT.

IN A LATRINE NEAR MOUNT MORRIS, HE READ A NEWSPAPER ACCOUNT OF MISS PATELLA'S RECENTLY ANNOUNCED WORLD FAREWELL TOUR.

THE THIRD IN RECENT MEMORY.

IN THIS BUSINESSMAN, CUT OFF FROM NORMAL FAMILY RELATIONS, MISS PATELLA HAD FOUND HER PERFECT ADMIRER.

AFTER FORTY YEARS ON THE STAGE, IT IS TIME FOR ME TO BID ADIEU TO MY DEVOTED AUDIENCE."

PLANS WERE BEING SET FOR HER TO MAKE A FINAL VISIT TO NORTH AMERICA.

"TO CAST MY EYES FOR ONE LAST TIME ON THE MIGHTY NIAGARA FALLS; TO WALK THE STREETS OF NEW YORK ONCE AGAIN..."

A CRINOLINE-EATING ALLIGATOR.

MISS PATELLA AS FLORIDA IN THE FLUME OF YOUTH

HERE WAS AN OTHERWISE CANNY BUSINESSMAN TAKEN IN COMPLETELY BY THIS THEATRICAL FRIPPERY.

HERE SHE IS AS THE CASTAWAY, ROLDINE, IN "WASHED-UP AND WARNED."

ANOTHER MALE ROLE?

The Renowned Actress Miss PATELLA IN WASHED-UP & WARNED

WITH TEARS IN HIS EYES, HE RECOUNTED THE STORY OF HOW MISS PATELLA LOST HER RIGHT LEG THROUGH THE NEGLECT OF A GANGRENOUS WOUND.

SHE IS CARRIED FROM COACH TO THEATER IN THE ARMS OF HER FAITHFUL SERVANT.

YET IN EVERY PRINT HE SHOWED ME, SHE POSSESSED ALL OF HER LIMBS.

YES, ISN'T IT WONDERFUL?

AS WE WERE BOTH DESCENDED FROM A COMMON ANCESTRAL SPRING, I WOULD OFTEN, AS A FORM OF SMALL TALK OR INNOCENT GAME, TRY TO ESTABLISH A DIRECT FAMILIAL CONNECTION WITH MR. KETZELBOURD.

I HAD A COUSIN, TWICE REMOVED, IN AMSTERDAM WHO, I BELIEVE, MARRIED A KETZELBOURD.

AH, LOOK!

THEIR ONLY SON IMMIGRATED TO BARBADOS IN 1813.

YOU CAN SEE THERE, THROUGH THE TREES, THE ROOFS OF THE LIVONIA INSANE ASYLUM.

IN THESE GAMES, HE HAD NO INTEREST.

IT IS SAID, "EVERY MORNING MAN BECOMES A NEW CREATURE, AND FOR THIS HE HAS TO THANK GOD, BLESSED BE HE, WITH ALL HIS HEART."

ON A DAILY BASIS — MORNING, NOON AND NIGHT — HE PUT ASIDE HIS WORLDLY PURSUITS AND RETREATED INTO THE PRIVACY OF AN IMAGINED SANCTUARY.

IF MR. DELLA ROBBIA CAN'T WAIT, TELL HIM THAT HIS OLD MUSK SACS CAN BE CAUTERIZED BY ANY LOCAL BLACKSMITH.

IMAGINE THESE CRUDE REPRESENTATIONS ELICITING SUCH FERVENT ADORATION FROM AN OTHERWISE REASONABLE MAN.

CRUDE? IN WHAT WAY? I'D HAVE TO SEE FOR MYSELF.

THERE, IN THE COMPANY OF HIS PRINTS, HE WOULD OFTEN AND WANTONLY SPILL HIS SEED.

"MAN ANSWERS HIS OWN PRAYERS THROUGH ACTION IN THIS WORLD."

I WILL NEVER KNOW WHETHER HIS USE OF THESE IMAGES WAS PART OF A PAGAN RITUAL OR MERELY SOME CULTISH ACCESSORY IN THE WORSHIP OF GOD.

YOU SAY HE WAS A BAPTISED JEW, OR WAS IT A JEWISH BAPTIST?

IN ANY CASE, TO WORSHIP GOD WITH RITES THAT ARE NOT PRESCRIBED BY LAW IS AN ACT OF IDOLATRY. HOW CAN YOU COMPARE THESE LEWD IMAGES TO THE CHERUBIM EMBROIDERED ON THE CURTAINS OF OUR TABERNACLE?

ANOTHER ROUND OF OYSTERS, GENTLEMEN?

A FEW ROCKS WERE ARRANGED IN THE FORM OF AN ALTAR TO HOLD HIS COLLECTION OF PICTURES OF MISS PATELLA.

AS VENUS IN "BATHWATER LOST," AS CAPT. MARCUS IN "THE PUBLIC TONSIL," AS SISTER FLOREAL IN "THE MADMAN'S HOMECOMING," AND AS STORIETTE IN "TITAN'S CRACKER."

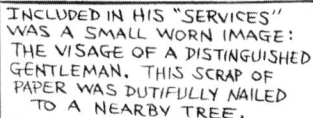

INCLUDED IN HIS "SERVICES" WAS A SMALL WORN IMAGE: THE VISAGE OF A DISTINGUISHED GENTLEMAN. THIS SCRAP OF PAPER WAS DUTIFULLY NAILED TO A NEARBY TREE.

THE MAN IN WHOSE PRESENCE THIS RITUAL WAS PERFORMED EACH DAY WAS, I DISCOVERED, THE GREAT JOHN JACOB ASTOR.

RIBBONO SHEL OLAM!

THANKFULLY, HE DID NOT PROSELYTIZE OR IN ANY WAY TRY TO INCLUDE ME IN THESE CEREMONIES.

"BLESSED BE HE WHO HATH UPROOTED IDOLATRY FROM OUR LAND, AND AS IT HAS BEEN UPROOTED FROM THIS PLACE, SO MIGHT IT BE UPROOTED FROM ALL PLACES BELONGING TO ISRAEL; AND DO THOU TURN THE HEART OF THOSE THAT SERVE THEM [THE PAGAN GODS] TO SERVE THEE."

IT'S AN ALL-GIRL'S PANTOGRAPH ACADEMY.

IN THE MOST REMOTE VILLAGES WE VISITED, THERE WERE AMPLE OPPORTUNITIES TO ENJOY FEMALE SOCIETY.

MISS FLOX BELIEVES THAT THE AMERICAN WOMAN MUST BE EMANCIPATED FIRST—THE AFRICAN SLAVE WILL FOLLOW HER EXAMPLE.

THAT IS, IF THE AMERICAN BUSINESSMAN FINDS NO OBJECTION.

BUT AT THE END OF THE EVENING, KETZELBOURD RETURNED TO HIS PAPER-AND-INK REPRESENTATIONS.

PEW! MY CLOTHING REEKS OF A HUNDRED FRENCH PERFUMES.

THESE WERE SIMPLE WOOD ENGRAVINGS; WORKMANLIKE COPIES OF COPIES OF THE MOST CONVENTIONALIZED IMAGES OF WOMANKIND, PRINTED IN BLACK INK.

I BOUGHT THIS ONE OFF A DUTCH PEDDLER IN UTICA. THE IDIOT TRIMMED IT DOWN TO FIT IN A MOCK TORTOISE-SHELL FRAME.

AN ASSEMBLAGE OF CONVEX LINES—FAR REMOVED FROM ANY FIRST-HAND OBSERVATIONS FROM NATURE—DESCRIBING LIMBS, TORSO, AND HEAD.

THIS SERIES OF MISS PATELLA IN "ARTEMIS AT BUNKER HILL" FELL INTO MY HANDS BY SHEER LUCK. A STATIONER STRICKEN WITH PALSY HAD TO LIQUIDATE HIS STOCK.

SOME EXAMPLES WERE HAND-TINTED, WITH THE AID OF STENCILS, IN A LIMITED PALATE OF SEMI-OPAQUE COLORS: SPOILED-SALMON PINK, INDAMINE BLUE, VERDIGRIS GREEN, CRESOL RED AND MASSICOT YELLOW.

IT WAS HER HUSBAND, OF ALL PEOPLE, WHO SUGGESTED THAT NOAH WRITE A PLAY FOR HER—A PATRIOTIC DRAMA—AND BEFORE YOU KNOW IT, THEY'RE DALLYING HER ON THEIR COLLECTIVE KNEE.

THE COLORS ONLY APPROXIMATELY OVERLAID THE FORMS THEY WERE ASSIGNED TO—THE PRODUCT OF POORLY PAID PIECEWORK DONE BY A CHILD OR CARELESS ADULT.

LOOK AT THE SILVER TINSEL ON HER QUIVER.

TO MAKE THE LEAP OF SENSORIAL ASSOCIATION FROM THESE CRUDE PRINTS TO THE FLESH OF AN ACTUAL WOMAN REQUIRED A RECKLESS IMAGINATION.

THAT MISS FLOX IS QUITE A FLIRT.

THE TRAILS WE FOLLOWED BORE A HEAVY TRAFFIC OF TRAPPERS, DISPLACED INDIANS, LAND SURVEYORS, PEDDLERS, MANU-MITTED SLAVES AND RELIGIOUS ZEALOTS.

HE WEARS A NUMBER 7 WEASEL TRAP ON HIS THIGH IN PENANCE FOR SOME SIN HE COMMITTED IN SYRACUSE.

WE TRAVELED LIGHT: OUR INVENTORY OF TRAPS, POLES AND KNIVES, OUR PAYMENTS RECEIVED, AND EVEN MY SALARY RESIDED IN A NOTEBOOK.

ON PAPER? NO! THESE FIGURES REPRESENT ACTUAL PELTS TRANSFERRED FROM ONE ROOM OF A WAREHOUSE IN ALBANY TO ANOTHER. A DUPLICATE OF THIS LEDGER IS KEPT IN THE FIRST NATIONAL BANK OF UTICA — SAFE AND SOUND.

THE SABBATH CAME AND WENT UNNOTICED.

NATURE CAN'T AFFORD TO TAKE A DAY OFF WORK AND EITHER CAN I.

AND THEN, IN THE FLOODING OF SOME NAMELESS RIVER, THE TRUNK, CONTAINING MY TEFILLIN AND OTHER CHERISHED POSSESSIONS, WAS LOST.

WHO CARRIES SUCH THINGS ON THEIR PERSON? IN LIMA, WE PASSED A REPUTABLE BANK WITH SAFE DEPOSIT BOXES!

AS I WAS FORCED BY CIRCUMSTANCE TO TEM-PORARILY ABANDON MY OWN RELIGIOUS OBSERVANCES, I WAS TOLERANT OF HIS.

HERE'S MISS PATELLA AS VIRGILINA, THE BLIND GIRL, STRAPPED TO A RUNAWAY PONY CART IN ASTART'S "PHLEGMATICUS."

THE MOST COMMON RELIC OF THE ANCIENT WORLD IS THAT OF A TINY FEMALE FIGURE STAMPED IN CLAY. ITS WORSHIPERS HOPED TO SOMEHOW INFLUENCE THEIR SUCCESS IN PLANTING, HUNTING OR WHATEVER. TODAY, WE FIND IT EVERYWHERE IN THE NEAR EAST. IT CAN BE HAD BY COLLECTORS FOR A FEW DOLLARS.

OUR WINTERS WERE SPENT IN A SUCCESSION OF HOTELS AND BOARDING HOUSES, BUT I HAD ALREADY DEVELOPED A PREFERENCE FOR SLEEPING IN THE OUT-OF-DOORS.

YOU'LL BE CHARGED FOR THE BED ALL THE SAME!

MAYBE I COULD INTEREST YOU IN A NEW SET OF PHYLACTERIES — BEAUTIFUL, GOLD-STAMPED, THE HIGHEST QUALITY.

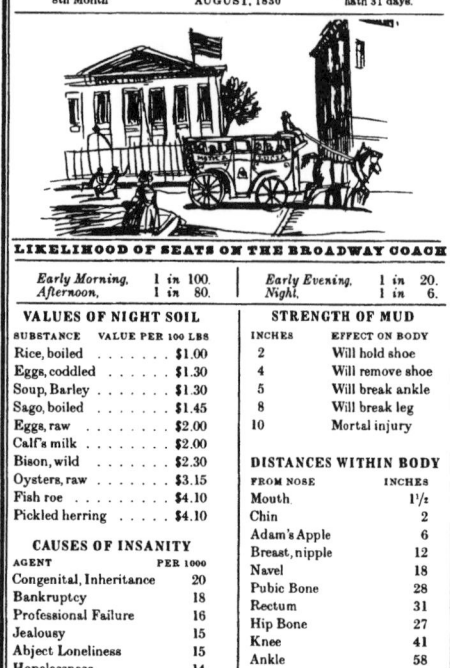

8th Month AUGUST, 1830 hath 31 days.

LIKELIHOOD OF SEATS ON THE BROADWAY COACH

Early Morning,	1 in 100.	*Early Evening,*	1 in 20.
Afternoon,	1 in 80.	*Night,*	1 in 6.

VALUES OF NIGHT SOIL

SUBSTANCE	VALUE PER 100 LBS
Rice, boiled	$1.00
Eggs, coddled	$1.30
Soup, Barley	$1.30
Sago, boiled	$1.45
Eggs, raw	$2.00
Calf's milk	$2.00
Bison, wild	$2.30
Oysters, raw	$3.15
Fish roe	$4.10
Pickled herring	$4.10

CAUSES OF INSANITY

AGENT	PER 1000
Congenital, Inheritance	20
Bankruptcy	18
Professional Failure	16
Jealousy	15
Abject Loneliness	15
Hopelessness	14
Humiliation	12
Opium	9
Dancing	2

STRENGTH OF MUD

INCHES	EFFECT ON BODY
2	Will hold shoe
4	Will remove shoe
5	Will break ankle
8	Will break leg
10	Mortal injury

DISTANCES WITHIN BODY

FROM NOSE	INCHES
Mouth	1½
Chin	2
Adam's Apple	6
Breast, nipple	12
Navel	18
Pubic Bone	28
Rectum	31
Hip Bone	27
Knee	41
Ankle	58
Foot	61

*A box 24 inches long by 16 inches wide will hold seven salted piglets.

TEN MILLION MORE:

COMMERCIAL THOUGHTS

ON THE

RESURRECTION.

By Professor Freeman Ough

PUBLISHED BY THE

Half-Light Mission

Bowery, New York

1828

One Sheet 48 Periodical

No. 7.

VOL II
1830

THE

MONTHLY CISTERN,

AND LIBRARY OF

Spurious Knowledge.

HOW LITTLE WE KNOW — CARE — OR HONOR.

AUGUST, 1830

ILLUSTRATIONS.

Theater Alley at Midnight — A Hive of Rats and
Actors — A Drunkard.

CONTENTS.

NEW-YORK:
PUBLISHED BY JONAS PHULL.
96 Nile Street.

One Dollar per year in advance.

THE SHORT

Life

OF

A RESTAURANT HABITUE

BY A. CADAVER

PUBLISHED BY

THE SECOND WIND SOCIETY

BOSTON

AS THE WINTER SNOWS BEGAN TO RECEDE, WE DISCOVERED THAT THE FOREST FLOOR WAS LITTERED WITH CHEAPLY PRINTED RELIGIOUS TRACTS.

"'BURNT OFFERINGS FOR DEWY-EYED YOUTHS,' BY REV. C. MEDLEY."

"'FROM DUNGHILL TO EXECUTIVE MANSION,' BY PYRON FOLD.'"

LIMPCOVER EDITIONS, PAMPHLETS, CHAPBOOKS, CATECHISMS IN REBUS FORM, ONE-VOLUME ILLUSTRATED HISTORIES OF THE WORLD SINCE CREATION, CHILDREN'S BIBLES...

THEY MUST'VE BEEN THROUGH HERE IN LATE AUTUMN.

"'TWENTY YEARS OF BUSINESS CORRE-SPONDENCE WITH THE BRAZEN SERPENT,' BY MORRIS COSECANT."

SONGBOOKS, CHURCH ORGANS, ALMANACS, CONFESSIONAL BIOGRAPHIES, FAMILY PICTORIAL REVIEWS AND COLLECTIONS OF MORALISTIC ANIMAL FABLES — ALL WATER STAINED BUT STILL LEGIBLE.

"'THE SHORT LIFE OF A RESTAURANT HABITUÉ,' BY A. CADAVER."

"'DRAUGHTS FROM THE PAPAL CISTERN,' BY BROTHER OREFICI."

THERE ARE HIGH-SPEED STEAM PRESSES IN BOSTON AND NEW YORK SPEWING OUT MORE PRINTED MATERIAL THAN CAN EVER BE CONSUMED — OVER THREE HUNDRED THOUSAND BIBLES AND SIX MILLION TRACTS LAST YEAR ALONE.

POOR BOYS HAVE BEEN ORGANIZED INTO COLPORTEUR BRIGADES. THEY'RE ARMED WITH PACKETS OF PRINTED MATERIAL AND CAN'T RETURN UNTIL THEY'VE DISCHARGED ALL OF THEIR AMMUNITION.

IT'S A WAR OF PAMPHLETEERS: UNITARIANS AGAINST EPISCOPALIANS, MODERATE LIGHT AGAINST NEW LIGHT — THEY'VE DRIVEN EVERYTHING ELSE OFF THE SHELVES!

"'THE OPOSSUM: FEIGNING DEATH IN LIFE,' BY CAPTAIN FISTIC."

"'TEN MILLION MORE: COMMERCIAL THOUGHTS ON THE RESURRECTION,' BY PROF. FREEMAN OUGHT, P.D."

"'THE FEMALE SHROUD, OR TIGHT STAYS ON THE SPIRIT BODY,' BY SISTER LILY VANDOR.'"

DO YOU KNOW WHAT IT COSTS TO IMPORT ONE FINELY PRINTED PASSOVER HAGGADAH FROM BERLIN?

IN ANY CASE, ON THOSE FIRST WARM NIGHTS OF SPRING, THIS LITERATURE PROVIDED US WITH SOMETHING TO READ.

"'WE OFFER BIBLICAL PROOF THAT THE CITIZENS OF THE UNITED STATES ARE THE CHOSEN PEOPLE AND THAT THIS GREAT CONTINENT WILL BE THE SCENE OF THE SECOND COMING.'"

IN THE AUTUMN OF OUR THIRD YEAR TOGETHER, AN OFFHAND REMARK BY A COCKY YOUNG TRAPPER PLUNGED KETZELBOURD INTO A PROFOUND STATE OF MELANCHOLIA.

THAT'S THE FIRST BEAVER I'VE SEEN SINCE ST. LOUIS.

HE WAS OVERCOME BY THE SUDDEN REALIZATION THAT THIS CREATURE, UPON WHOSE PELT HIS FORTUNE WAS BUILT, WAS NOW ON THE VERGE OF EXTERMINATION.

THEY SAY THEY'RE ALL BUT GONE EAST OF THE ROCKIES.

WHO EVER DREAMED THAT THE DEMAND FOR HATS WOULD ONE DAY OUTSTRIP THE POWERS OF ANIMAL PROCREATION?

THE MELANCHOLIAC TENDS TO SEIZE UPON A GRANDIOSE CAUSE FOR HIS TERRIBLE SADNESS: THE FATE OF THE MOUNTAIN BEAVER, THE DESTRUCTION OF THE SECOND TEMPLE, THE FALL OF THE ROMAN EMPIRE. THE AFFLICTION ITSELF PREVENTS HIM FROM CONSIDERING THE MOST OBVIOUS FACTORS WHICH LIE CLOSE AT HAND: THE ROUTINES OF DAILY LIFE AND HIS OWN WEAKENED CONSTITUTION.

NOT TO MENTION THE DEBILITATING EFFECTS OF CHRONIC IDOL WORSHIP.

FOR A FULL SIX MONTHS HE MOURNED. THE DAY-TO-DAY BUSINESS OF LEASING TRAPS AND OTHER EQUIPMENT WAS LEFT TO ME.

WHO DIED?

HIS HAT.

2,537 MATURE PELTS TAKEN FROM APRIL TO JUNE OF 1824.

HIS DAYS WERE SPENT IN A CEASELESS FRENZY OF MEMORIAL ORATION. HE DWELT AT LENGTH UPON THE TRAGIC INEVITABILITY OF THE BEAVER'S EXTINCTION, NEVER MENTIONING THE PART HE PLAYED IN IT.

IT WAS A SOCIAL ANIMAL — THAT WAS ITS DOWNFALL. THE REGULARITY OF ITS COMINGS AND GOINGS MADE IT AN EASY MARK.

WITH HIS UNWASHED FINGERS, HE HELD, FOR DEAR LIFE, HIS PLACE IN THE PAGES OF AN OLD NATURAL HISTORY PRIMER.

"IN THIS AQUATIC ANIMAL, THE WOOF OF INSTINCT HAS BEEN EXQUISITELY INTERWOVEN WITH THE WARP OF PURPOSEFUL REASON."

AT NIGHT, ONE NO LONGER HEARD THE SPLASHING OF BEAVERS AT WORK — ONLY HIS PATHETIC SOBS.

WHOoo... WHOoo... HUT, HUT, HUT...

HE PROPOSED THAT HENCEFORTH ALL BUSINESS BE SUSPENDED ON APRIL 15th IN COMMEMORATION OF THE FEMALE BEAVER'S YEARLY ESTROUS CYCLE —

AT THIS TIME OF YEAR, THEIR NIPPLES INCREASE IN SIZE, THEIR VULVA SWELL AND THEY BEGIN, SPONTANEOUSLY, TO OVULATE.

A SOLEMN DAY OF NATIONAL REMORSE FOR OPPORTUNITIES LOST.

THE FEMALE MAY THEORETICALLY BE IN "HEAT" A FULL TWO WEEKS, BUT IS ONLY RECEPTIVE TO OVERTURES FROM THE MALE FOR A BRIEF TEN- TO TWELVE-HOUR PERIOD — AFTER THAT, IT'S TOO LATE.

ON ALL FOURS, HE WOULD FOLLOW A SHALLOW STREAM TO THE POINT OF A DAM AND THEN TRY TO PHYSICALLY INSINUATE HIMSELF INTO THE ABANDONED LODGE.

THEY SAY THERE ARE ONES LARGE ENOUGH TO ACCOMMODATE A GROWN MAN

SHAUL, OF THE SHEARITH BATSAL BURIAL SOCIETY, CAN TELL YOU SOMETHING OF THIS HYSTERICAL URGE TO IMPERSONATE THE DEARLY DEPARTED.

A WIDOW MIMICKING THE FAMILIAR EUPHEMISTIC OATHS OF HER LATE HUSBAND...

HANG IT! THIS SOUP IS COLD!

A NEPHEW ADOPTING WHOLESALE THE OPINIONS OF HIS DEAD UNCLE.

WHAT DOES THE BEY OF TUNIS CARE FOR MY WELL-BEING?

HIS EVENINGS WERE DEVOTED WITH RENEWED VIGOR TO THE RITUAL ADORATION OF MISS PATELLA.

TODAY, THE SCARCITY OF THE BEAVER HAS FORCED HATMAKERS TO ROUTINELY WORK THE "WOOL" OF OTHER CREATURES INTO THEIR SO-CALLED BEAVER HATS — MUSKRAT, NUSTRIMA, GALOPEAS AND OTHERS YOU'VE NEVER HEARD OF.

NATHAN, MY BOY, THE ITALIAN SILK CYLINDER IS NOW DE RIGUEUR IN THE CITY OF NEW YORK.

TODAY FRESH OYSTERS

ONE RAINY DAY, THAT SAME MONTH, HE STOPPED BEFORE AN UNREMARKABLE MOUND OF EARTH OVERGROWN WITH TENDER FOLIAGE.

AH, WHAT WE HAVE HERE IS A CASTORIUM PILE.

BY WAY OF EXPLANATION, HE BEGAN TO RE-ENACT THE METHOD OF ITS CONSTRUCTION WHILE PROVIDING A RUNNING COMMENTARY.

IN THE SPRING, THE BEAVER MAY FIND ITSELF WITH A SUPERABUNDANCE OF CASTORIUM: A MUSK-SCENTED OILY SUBSTANCE SECRETED BY AN ANAL GLAND.

HE WILL TRAVEL A SHORT DISTANCE, TO A POINT BETWEEN HIS LODGE AND THAT OF A NEIGHBOR'S, AND THERE, ON THE FOREST FLOOR, DEPOSIT A QUANTITY OF CASTORIUM. I CARRY MINE IN A JAR.

ANOTHER BEAVER, DRAWN BY THIS IRRESISTIBLE SCENT, WILL, IN AN ACT OF ONE-UPMANSHIP, COVER IT WITH EARTH AND LEAVES AND THEN MAKE HIS OWN DEPOSIT UPON THE ANOINTED SPOT.

AND SO ON, AND SO FORTH, THE MOUND WILL SLOWLY RISE TO A HEIGHT OF FOUR TO FIVE FEET: A MONUMENT TO THE POWERS OF THIS CURIOUS SUBSTANCE!

SNIF SNIF

AT SOME POINT, KETZEL-BOURD'S DEMONSTRATION LAPSED INTO A WORDLESS DISPLAY OF ANIMALISTIC BEHAVIOR.

HE FROLICKED IN THE MUD FOR HALF AN HOUR AND THEN SCURRIED TO A NEARBY STREAM TO WASH HIMSELF.

WITH HIS BARE FOOT, HE IMITATED THE SOUND OF A BEAVER'S TAIL SLAPPING THE SURFACE OF THE WATER — A WARNING TO OTHER BEAVERS OF DANGER.

ALAS, TOO LATE.

PLAT PLAT

IN THE SUMMER OF MY FOURTH YEAR IN THE WILDERNESS, WE CAME UPON A PECULIAR SETTLEMENT BUILT ON THE LEEWARD SIDE OF A GENTLY SLOPING HILL.

THE WORDS "NEW AFFLATUS" SPELT PHONETICALLY WITH HEBREW CHARACTERS!

WELCOME, WELCOME, I AM SEPTUM DANDY, PNEUMATIC PILOT AND ENGINEER, THIRD DEGREE. THESE ARE MY SONS, VAYU AND NOTUS; AND THIS IS MY SISTER-BRIDE, SUSPIRA.

OURS IS A COMMUNALISTIC SECT FOUNDED UPON THE SCIENTIFIC PRINCIPLES OF THE GREAT GENIUS AND DISCOVERER OF OXYGEN, JOSEPH PRIESTLY.

CALL US FREE OXYGENATORS, AIR BATHERS, WIND WORSHIPERS... IT'S ALL THE SAME TO US. OUR GOAL: TO SEE TO IT THAT THIS FREE AND MOST UBIQUITOUS GIFT OF THE NATURAL WORLD IS NOT TURNED INTO A TAWDRY COMMODITY TO BE BOUGHT AND SOLD IN THE MARKETPLACE.

WHEN YOU HAVE TIME, YOU CAN JOIN OUR STUDY GROUP.

"I HAVE BEEN SO HAPPY AS BY ACCIDENT TO HAVE HIT UPON A METHOD OF RESTORING AIR INJURED BY CANDLES, AND TO HAVE DISCOVERED ONE OF THE RESTORATIVES WHICH NATURE EMPLOYS, IT IS VEGETATION."

FROM THESE INCONTROVERTIBLE FACTS, THEY EXTRAPOLATED THE SCIENTIFIC DESTINY OF AMERICA.

WHEN THIS CONTINENT IS THOROUGHLY OXYGENATED, THERE WILL BE NO NEED FOR PERMANENT DWELLINGS. THE CITIZENS OF THE UNITED STATES WILL REASSUME THE SALUTARY WANDERING LIFE OF THE ANCIENT HEBREWS.

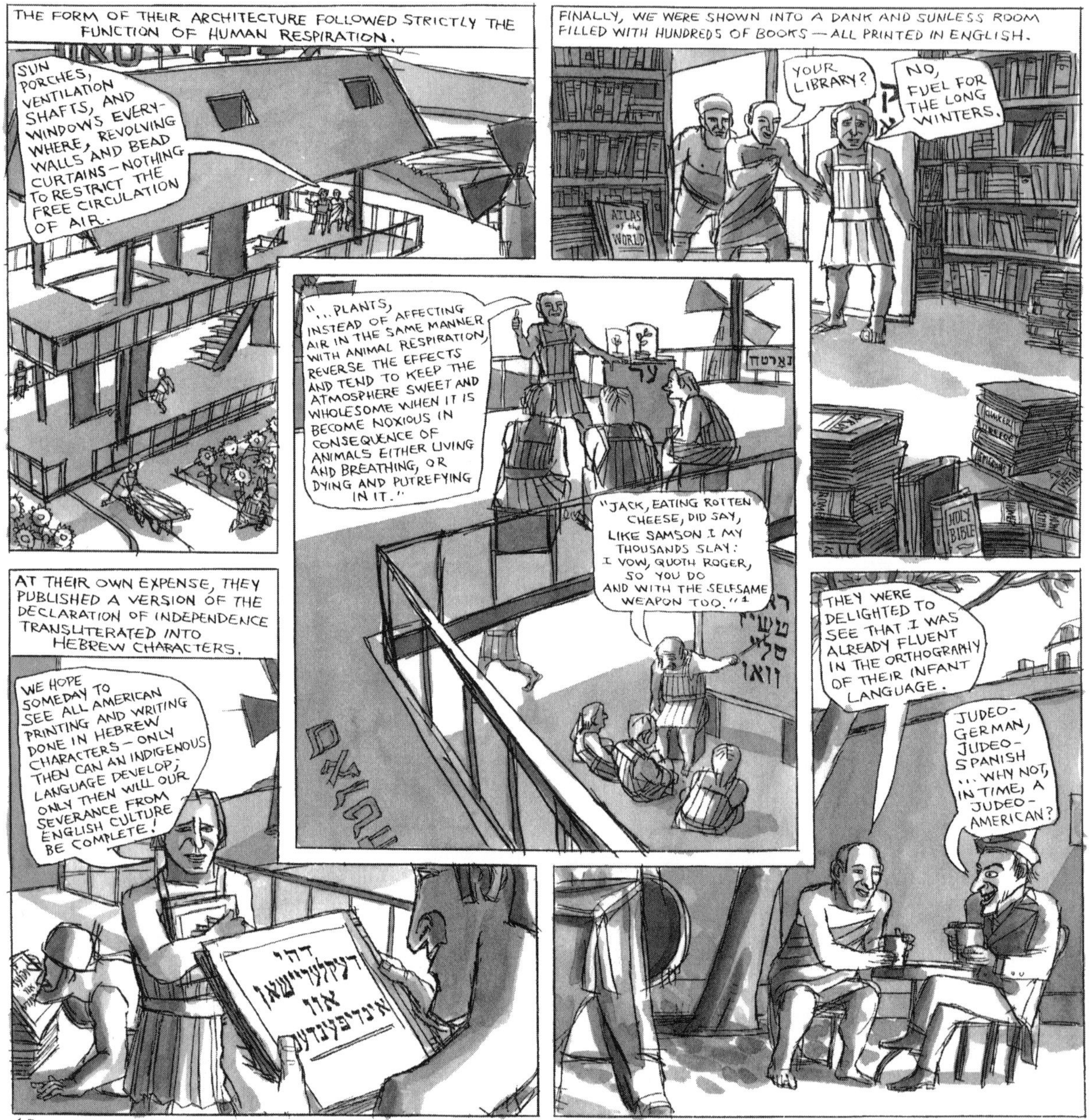
THE FORM OF THEIR ARCHITECTURE FOLLOWED STRICTLY THE FUNCTION OF HUMAN RESPIRATION.
SUN PORCHES, VENTILATION SHAFTS, AND WINDOWS EVERYWHERE, REVOLVING WALLS AND BEAD CURTAINS—NOTHING TO RESTRICT THE FREE CIRCULATION OF AIR.
FINALLY, WE WERE SHOWN INTO A DANK AND SUNLESS ROOM FILLED WITH HUNDREDS OF BOOKS—ALL PRINTED IN ENGLISH.
YOUR LIBRARY?
NO, FUEL FOR THE LONG WINTERS.
ATLAS of the WORLD
HOLY BIBLE
"...PLANTS, INSTEAD OF AFFECTING AIR IN THE SAME MANNER WITH ANIMAL RESPIRATION, REVERSE THE EFFECTS AND TEND TO KEEP THE ATMOSPHERE SWEET AND WHOLESOME WHEN IT IS BECOME NOXIOUS IN CONSEQUENCE OF ANIMALS EITHER LIVING AND BREATHING, OR DYING AND PUTREFYING IN IT."
"JACK, EATING ROTTEN CHEESE, DID SAY, LIKE SAMSON I MY THOUSANDS SLAY: I VOW, QUOTH ROGER, SO YOU DO AND WITH THE SELFSAME WEAPON TOO."[1]
AT THEIR OWN EXPENSE, THEY PUBLISHED A VERSION OF THE DECLARATION OF INDEPENDENCE TRANSLITERATED INTO HEBREW CHARACTERS.
WE HOPE SOMEDAY TO SEE ALL AMERICAN PRINTING AND WRITING DONE IN HEBREW CHARACTERS—ONLY THEN CAN AN INDIGENOUS LANGUAGE DEVELOP; ONLY THEN WILL OUR SEVERANCE FROM ENGLISH CULTURE BE COMPLETE!
THEY WERE DELIGHTED TO SEE THAT I WAS ALREADY FLUENT IN THE ORTHOGRAPHY OF THEIR INFANT LANGUAGE.
JUDEO-GERMAN, JUDEO-SPANISH ...WHY NOT, IN TIME, A JUDEO-AMERICAN?

[1] BENJAMIN FRANKLIN

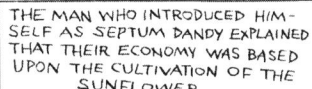

THE MAN WHO INTRODUCED HIM-SELF AS SEPTUM DANDY EXPLAINED THAT THEIR ECONOMY WAS BASED UPON THE CULTIVATION OF THE SUNFLOWER.

WE EAT ITS SEED, DRINK ITS OIL AND WEAVE OUR CLOTHING FROM ITS STALK. LET THE BEAVER CLOTHE ITSELF WITH ITS OWN FUR.

BY PROCESSING THE SEEDS WITH WIND-DRIVEN MACHINERY, WE ARE FREE TO SPEND OUR DAYS AIR-BATHING AND IN THE STUDY OF AESTHETICS.

THE SHELLS ARE "SPIT" FROM A ROOFTOP VENT DIRECTLY INTO A COMPOST HEAP.

WE READ THE NEWSPAPERS AND ARE AWARE OF THE TERRIBLE EPIDEMIC OF INSANITY THAT IS SWEEPING OVER THE NATION. MEN AND WOMEN LURED FROM THEIR SELF-SUFFICIENT FAMILY HOME-STEAD — BY THE PERFECTION OF MANUFACTURED GOODS THAT THEY COULD NOT OTHER-WISE AFFORD — INTO THE LIFE OF A WAGE-EARNER IN THE CITY.

THEIR GRAND EXPECTATIONS ARE SOON DISPELLED. TO PAY THE RENT FOR AN ILL-VENTILATED ROOM ABOVE A GROG-SHOP, THEY ARE FORCED TO WORK FIFTEEN HOURS A DAY, SIX DAYS A WEEK. THEIR ONE DAY OF REST IS SPENT IN A LICENTIOUS HAZE OF ALCOHOL AND FRIVOLOUS ENTERTAINMENT. THEY HAVE UNWITTINGLY BECOME WAGE SLAVES: INSTRUMENTS IN THE ACCUMULATION OF CAPITAL FOR A HANDFUL OF FACELESS PLUTOCRATS.

THEY ARE TORTURED, DAY AND NIGHT, BY THE FEAR OF IMMINENT FAILURE. THEY KNOW THAT ECONOMIC FAILURE LEADS TO LONELINESS, DESTITUTION AND PRISON. MANY A TIME THEY'VE WATCHED HELPLESSLY AS THEIR LESS FORTUNATE ACQUAINTANCES CRASHED ON THE REEFS OF CAPITALISM. IS IT ANY WONDER THAT THE INSANE ASYLUMS ARE FILLED TO OVERFLOWING WITH THESE YOUNG GO-GETTERS?

AS PEOPLE ARE WONT TO DO IN TIMES OF PLAGUE, WE FLED THE CITY WITH ITS GLITTERING SHOW-ROOMS AND THEATERS, TO CAST OUR LOT WITH THE SIMPLE PLEASURES OF FRESH AIR. WE CHOSE THE PATH A CREATURE ENDOWED WITH TWO NOSTRILS MUST NATURALLY CHOOSE,

FROM OUR CLOTHING AND LACK OF POSSESSIONS THEY GATHERED THAT WE, TOO, IN OUR OWN WAY, HAD RENOUNCED THE MARKET ECONOMY.

FOR THE TIME BEING, YOU MAY SLEEP HERE, ON THE NORTH-NORTH-EASTERLY PORCH, WITH SISTER CILIA AND HER MOTHER.

[29]

DURING THOSE TEN MONTHS AT NEW AFFLATUS, KETZELBOURD CONTINUED HIS PRIVATE WORSHIP OF MISS PATELLA.

...AS LADY PISGAH IN "THE PROMISED LAND."

ACCORDING TO BROTHER DANDY, THE BURNING FOOTLIGHTS IN MOST THEATERS CREATE A NOXIOUS ATMOSPHERIC CONDITION.

BETWEEN COMPULSORY LECTURES ON THE LIFE OF PRIESTLY, HE WOULD SNEAK OFF WITH HIS PACKET OF THEATRICAL PRINTS.

ALTHOUGH HE NO LONGER MOURNED THE BEAVER, HE WAS SEEN ONE AFTERNOON ON THE MAIN LAWN STRIKING BESTIAL POSES: WALKING ON ALL FOURS, LICKING HIMSELF AND BATHING IMMODESTLY IN A REFLECTING POOL.

SLAP SLAP

A WEEK LATER, I WAS CAUGHT SLAUGHTERING A WILD TURKEY.

FOR SPORT, OF COURSE, I'M NOT HUNGRY.

WE WERE SUMMONED BEFORE THE COMMITTEE OF HIGH VENTILATORS...

DURING THIS BRIEF PROBATIONARY PERIOD, YOU HAVE BOTH OPENLY ENGAGED IN CRUEL AND INDECENT BEHAVIOR — SOME UNFORTUNATE RESIDUE OF YOUR FORMER LIVES STILL CLINGS TO YOU.

AND ENCOURAGED TO LEAVE.

BUT EVEN HERE, WE MUST FOLLOW CERTAIN GENTLE PRECEPTS.

KETZELBOURD WENT ON, I THINK, TOWARD THE WEST IN SEARCH OF LIVING BEAVERS; I, BY CHANCE, MET A CANAL-BOAT AGENT SELLING EASTBOUND TICKETS AT A REDUCED PRICE.

DO YOU SUFFER FROM A

DISEASE

or Disorder of the Brain and Nervous System?

SELFISHNESS.	PERVERSITY.
DYSPEPSIA.	PASSION.
AVARICE.	HYSTERIA.
HYPOCHONDRIA.	EPILEPSY.
MANIA.	ALCOHOLISM.
SPERMATORRHOEA.	NEURASTHENIA.

All of these afflictions, and others too numerous to mention, have been treated with some degree of success at

DR. EMIL VINYACK'S

COMPULSORY HOTEL

& LUNATIC ASYLUM.

LOCATED 20 MILES FROM ALBANY, NEW YORK.

On your next business trip, make a point of touring our Hotel Grounds and Medical Facilities.

WE ARE AFFILIATED WITH NO OTHER INSTITUTION OR MEDICAL SOCIETY.

DR. VINYACK'S OLEO-CURE IS A PATENTED PROCEDURE AVAILABLE NOWHERE ELSE IN NORTH AMERICA.

Vinyack's Compulsory Hotel & Lunatic Asylum.

OROMELO, NEW YORK.

EW AFFLATUS

DECLARATION OF INDEPENDENCE

דהי
דעקלעריישאן
און
אינדיפענדענס

הוועז אין דהי קורס און היומען איוועני
events human of course the in When
איט ביקאמס נעסעסערי פאר וואן פיפל
people one for necessary becomes it
דיזאלוו דהי פאוליטיקעל בענדס הוויט
which bands political the dissolve
העוו קאנעקטעד דהעם ווידה עגאדהער,
,another with them connected have
טו עסיום עמאנג דהי פאוערס און דהי
the of powers the among assume to
אירטה דהי סעפערייט ענד איקוועל סט
on equal and separate the earth
טו הוויטש דהי לאז און נייטשור, ענד
and ,nature of laws the which to
און נייטשרס גאד, ענטאייטל דהעם, ע
a ,them entitle ,God nature's of
דיסענט ריספעקט טו דהי אופיניאנס או
of opinions the to respect decent
מענקאיינד ריקוואיירס דהעט דהיי שוד
should they that requires mankind
דיקלער דהי קאזס הוויטש אימפעל
impel which causes the declare
דהעם טו דהי סעפריישאן.
.separation the to them

YOSL FEINBROYT, A LATTER-DAY DISCIPLE OF THE FAMOUS KABBALIST AND VAGRANT, ABRAHAM ABULAFIA, SPENDS HIS AFTERNOONS IN THE CHALDEAN GARDENS.

"CHOOSE A LONELY HOUSE WHERE NONE SHALL HEAR THY VOICE!"

CHALDEAN GARDENS

IN THIS QUIET ENCLOSURE HE IS ABLE TO HEAR AND TRANSCRIBE, INTO ENGLISH, THE SOUNDS OF EATING AND DRINKING.

ALL LANGUAGES ARE BUT A CORRUPTION OF THE ABORIGINAL LANGUAGE — HEBREW!

ZHALOUP

GLUK

THESE COMBINATIONS OF LETTERS WHICH LIE OUTSIDE OF HUMAN LANGUAGE ARE LESS LIKELY TO DISTRACT FROM THE HARMONIOUS MOVEMENT OF PURE THOUGHT —

AND SO I WORKED WITH HIM FOR FIVE YEARS.

ZHALOUP

THE WORK OF A MIND WHICH HAS SEVERED ALL RELATIONS TO THE SENSES.

"THEN TAKE INK, PEN AND TABLET TO THY HAND AND REMEMBER THAT THOU ART ABOUT TO SERVE GOD IN JOY OF THE GLADNESS OF HEART."

ZHALOUP

"NOW BEGIN TO COMBINE A FEW OR MANY LETTERS, TO PERMUTE AND TO COMBINE THEM UNTIL THY HEART BE WARM."

SKINNING ANIMALS, DRESSING FURS... I HAD A FEELING FOR THAT SORT OF WORK

CHOUP

ZHA

"...AND WHEN THOU SEEST THAT BY COMBINATIONS OF LETTERS THOU CANST GRASP NEW THINGS WHICH BY HUMAN TRADITIONS OR BY THYSELF THOU WOULDST NOT BE ABLE TO KNOW..."

BUT FIVE YEARS IN THE WILDERNESS WAS LONG ENOUGH

AH!

ZHALOUP CHOL

"...AND WHEN THOU ART THUS PREPARED TO RECEIVE THE INFLUX OF DIVINE POWER WHICH FLOWS INTO THEE,"

GREPTS

SUCH ISOLATION BREEDS TERRIBLE OBSESSIONS. IT'S UNHEALTHY.

ZHALOUP CHOUP

"THEN TURN ALL THY TRUE THOUGHTS TO IMAGINE THE NAME AND HIS EXALTED ANGELS IN THY HEART AS IF THEY WERE HUMAN BEINGS SITTING OR STANDING ABOUT THEE."

COME. LET'S GO. WHERE ARE YOUR TROUSERS?

NATHAN KISHON RETURNS TO THE GIBRALTAR HOTEL ACCOMPANIED BY HIS FRIEND, MR. MARAH.

MY TROUSERS ARE IN ROOM 12.

OVER THE PAST FIVE YEARS I TOOK MY SALARY IN THE FORM OF BEAVER PELTS— A COMMODITY WHOSE VALUE HAS RECENTLY QUADRUPLED.

THE BEAVER IS MORE THAN WILLING TO HAVE ITS SOUL WITHDRAWN FROM THIS FURRY SHEATH.

HOW MUCH WOULD YOU SAY THEY'RE WORTH?

YOSL FEINBROYT LEAVES THE CHALDEAN GARDENS.

HE COMES HERE EVERY DAY. IT'S AN ECSTATIC TRANCE.

IN VELVET SLIPPERS, HE ASCENDS A LUMINOUS STAIRCASE EMBLAZONED WITH STRANGELY FAMILIAR WORDS OF NO EARTHLY LANGUAGE.

AT THE END OF A PALATIAL HALL HANGS A DELICATE CURTAIN EMBROIDERED WITH ONE UNDERSTANDABLE WORD—

A CRUDE, ONOMATOPOEIC REPRESENTATION OF THE ETERNAL SOUND OF RELIEF.

GREPTS

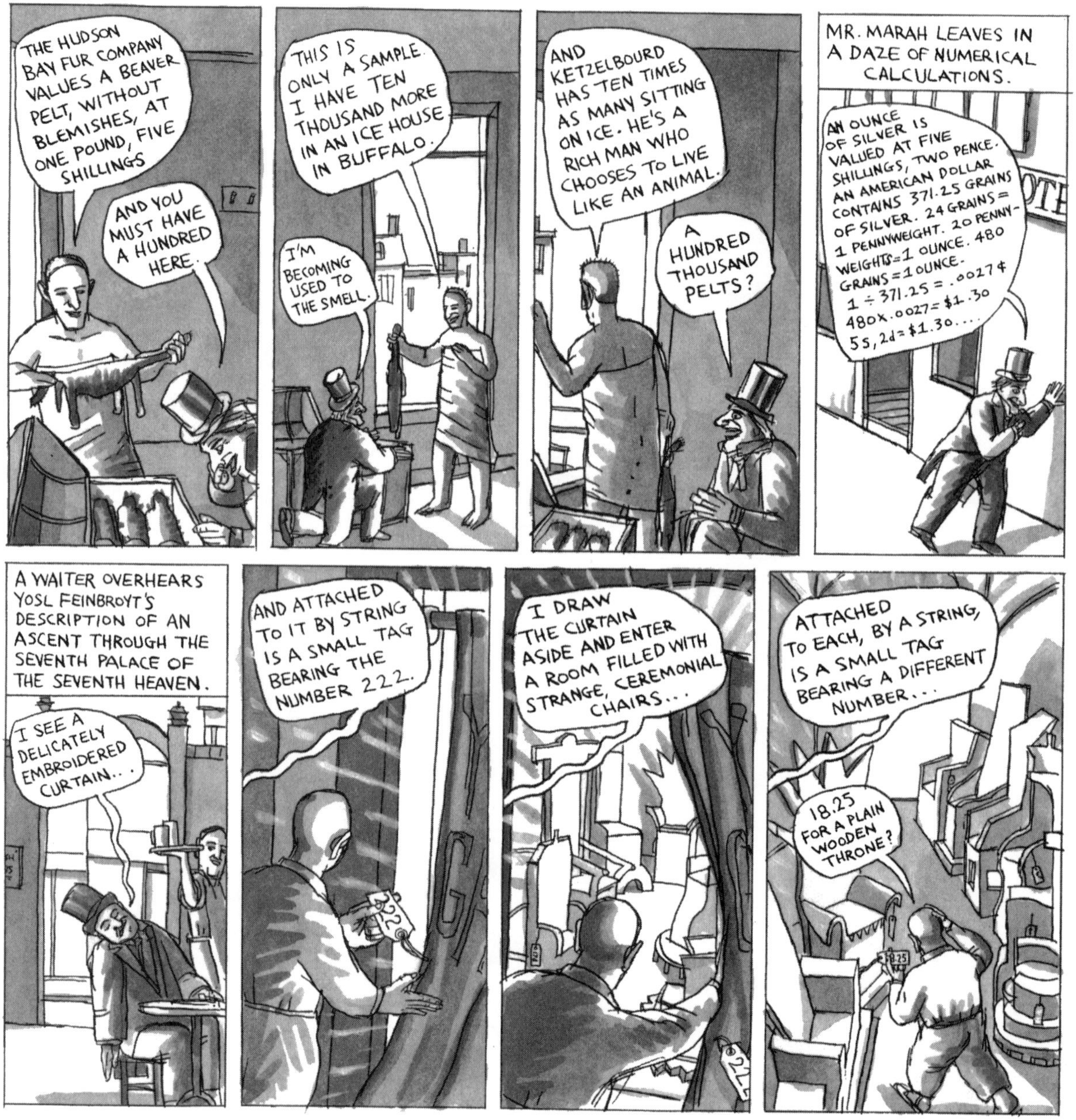
THE HUDSON BAY FUR COMPANY VALUES A BEAVER PELT, WITHOUT BLEMISHES, AT ONE POUND, FIVE SHILLINGS
AND YOU MUST HAVE A HUNDRED HERE.
THIS IS ONLY A SAMPLE. I HAVE TEN THOUSAND MORE IN AN ICE HOUSE IN BUFFALO.
I'M BECOMING USED TO THE SMELL.
AND KETZELBOURD HAS TEN TIMES AS MANY SITTING ON ICE. HE'S A RICH MAN WHO CHOOSES TO LIVE LIKE AN ANIMAL.
A HUNDRED THOUSAND PELTS?
MR. MARAH LEAVES IN A DAZE OF NUMERICAL CALCULATIONS.
AN OUNCE OF SILVER IS VALUED AT FIVE SHILLINGS, TWO PENCE. AN AMERICAN DOLLAR CONTAINS 371.25 GRAINS OF SILVER. 24 GRAINS = 1 PENNYWEIGHT. 20 PENNYWEIGHTS = 1 OUNCE. 480 GRAINS = 1 OUNCE. 1 ÷ 371.25 = .0027¢ 480x.0027 = $1.30 5s, 2d = $1.30....
A WAITER OVERHEARS YOSL FEINBROYT'S DESCRIPTION OF AN ASCENT THROUGH THE SEVENTH PALACE OF THE SEVENTH HEAVEN.
I SEE A DELICATELY EMBROIDERED CURTAIN...
AND ATTACHED TO IT BY STRING IS A SMALL TAG BEARING THE NUMBER 222.
222
I DRAW THE CURTAIN ASIDE AND ENTER A ROOM FILLED WITH STRANGE, CEREMONIAL CHAIRS...
222
ATTACHED TO EACH, BY A STRING, IS A SMALL TAG BEARING A DIFFERENT NUMBER...
18.25 FOR A PLAIN WOODEN THRONE?
18.25

A TWIG, SNAPPED BY THE WIND FROM AN OVER-HANGING BOUGH, AWAKENS YOSL FEINBROYT FROM A DEEP ECSTATIC TRANCE.

HE IMMEDIATELY BEGINS TO RECORD HIS IMPRESSIONS OF HIS RECENT CELESTIAL JOURNEY.

A FEW WORDS IN AN ANGELIC SCRIPT...

SHEETS OF PAPER ARE FILLED WITH INTRICATE DESIGNS AND FIGURES OF AN ESOTERIC NATURE.

YES! I REMEMBER!

EVEN A MAN WITH ONE FOOT OUT OF THIS WORLD MUST EAT AND PAY RENT

CHALDEAN GARDENS

AND SO, HE SELLS SOME OF THESE DRAWINGS TO A LOCAL EMBROIDERY HOUSE

1827 GOUPLE BROS. EMBROIDERED GOODS — OF ALL KINDS — FANCY WORK DRY GOODS

WHERE THEY ARE USED AS PATTERNS FOR THE ORNAMENTATION OF MEN'S HANDKERCHIEFS.

DURING THE SUMMER OF 1830, THESE 'KABBALAH STYLE' HANDKERCHIEFS REACHED THEIR HEIGHT OF POPULARITY IN NEW YORK CITY.

GOOD AFTERNOON. I REPRESENT THE KISHON FUR COMPANY OF BUFFALO, NY.

AH...

CHOO!

GESUNDHEIT

HIS HEART QUIVERING WITH EXCITEMENT, MR. MARAH CLIMBS TO THE SECOND-STORY SHOWROOM OF AN IMPORTER OF SPECIALTY DRY GOODS.

I'VE BEEN FLIRTING WITH THIS IDEA FOR SEVERAL MONTHS, BUT NOW IT'S TIME TO ACT.

CHAS. LORGNETTE CONTINENTAL DRY GOODS IMPORTS

GOOD AFTERNOON,

I HAVE SOMETHING NEW FROM PARIS — 20-DENIER SILK FLESHINGS IN FOUR NATURAL COLORS: ALABASTER, IVORY, PEACH AND GOOSEFLESH. WE ALREADY HAVE STANDING ORDERS FROM SEVERAL THEATERS IN PHILADELPHIA.

AND IF YOU HAVE ANY MORAL QUALMS ABOUT THIS SORT OF MERCHANDISE, YOU CAN READ HERE, FOR YOURSELF, A TRACTATE ON THE SUBJECT BY THE EMINENT FRENCH RABBI, JOSEF OLLVEYS OF TOULOUSE.

HMM?

"YOUR RECENT INVENTION OF AN ARTIFICIAL EPIDERMIS OR SECOND SKIN IS OF GREAT INTEREST TO THE JEWISH COMMUNITY. FROM TIME IMMEMORIAL, PUBLIC NAKEDNESS HAS BEEN SEEN AS A FORM OF PAGAN INDECENCY. IN THE MIDRASH, WE READ OF A MAN WHO UNCOVERED A WOMAN'S HEAD IN THE STREET. RABBI AKIVA ORDERED THAT HE PAY THE WOMAN 400 SILVER PIECES AS COMPENSATION FOR THE GREAT EMBARRASSMENT HE CAUSED HER..."

CARE FOR ONE?

THANK YOU.

THEY'RE MY FAVORITE.

DISCOUNT & SONS CO. CASTOR & POLLUX 48 LOZENGES 48 COUNT

YES, YES, PUT ME DOWN FOR 700 PAIRS. YOU'LL HAVE A BANK DRAFT ON WEDNESDAY.

AH, CORNERING THE MARKET?

AND HERE, AN INFORMAL STATEMENT FROM A NEW LIGHT DEACON IN ROCHESTER, NEW YORK, WHO CANNOT USE HIS NAME,

"AS THERE IS NOTHING MORE ABOMINABLE IN THE SIGHT OF GOD THAN THE MAN, OR WOMAN, WHO CAVORTS NAKED IN PUBLIC, YOUR NEW-STYLE FLESHINGS FILL AN URGENT NEED IN THE SPHERE OF PUBLIC DECENCY. I SINCERELY BELIEVE THAT THESE GARMENTS OFFER US THE WONDERFUL OPPORTUNITY OF TRANSFORMING LEWD THEATRICAL DISPLAY INTO EDIFYING ENTERTAINMENT.

CHARGED WITH A STRANGE NERVOUS ENERGY, MR. MARAH WALKS TOWARD LOWER BROADWAY.

I FEEL A FIRE IN MY LOINS— THE HEAT OF FREE ENTERPRISE!

AH, A FORTUNATE COINCIDENCE! THE BEAUTEOUS MISS PATELLA—KNOWN FOR HER REVEALING PERFORMANCES— BACK, ONCE AGAIN, IN TOWN.

NEW WORLD THEATER

PATELLA WORLD FAREWELL TOUR IN THE JEW OF NEW YORK SEPT. 10 THRU 24

I CAN SOLICIT HER IN PERSON WITH A SAMPLE PAIR OF THESE NEW FLESHINGS. WITH EVENING AND MATINEE PERFORMANCES, SHE MUST GO THROUGH A DOZEN PAIR EACH WEEK.

THOSE WERE TASTY DROPS MR. LORGNETTE GAVE ME. I SHOULD BRING SOME HOME FOR SARAH.

"CASTOR AND POLLUX DROPS"? YES, I KEEP THEM HERE FOR MARRIED GENTLEMEN.

95% PURE CASTOREUM EXTRACT IN A GLYCERIN BASE. A POTENT MALE RESTORATIVE, MY FRIEND, NOT AN AFTER-DINNER MINT.

CASTOREUM?

YES, AN OIL SECRETED BY THE ANAL GLAND OF THE ADULT MALE BEAVER. TWENTY-FOUR BEAVERS ARE REQUIRED TO MAKE ONE TIN OF THESE DROPS. GUARANTEED.

THE SOUND OF A DRUM BEAT TO AN EVER-MOUNTING TEMPO.

A GANG OF SHAME-FACED STREET BOYS RUN FOR COVER...

FOLLOWED BY A GUST OF WIND BEARING OLD BED RAGS AND OTHER PRIVATE DEBRIS,

MR. MARAH TAKES SHELTER IN THE DOORWAY OF A CHINA SHOP.

THAT'S THE FOURTH RALLY THIS WEEK.

THE PARADE TURNS ONTO PARK ROW.

I KNEW THIS BEHAVIOR WENT ON AMONGST IDLE YOUTHS, BUT I HAD NO IDEA OF ITS EXTENT OF ITS PRACTICE WITHIN THE GENERAL POPULACE.

IT THREATENS TO UNDERMINE THE NATION'S ECONOMY.

AN ENTIRE WORLD OF CUSTOMERS IS LOST TO US EACH DAY THROUGH THIS WASTEFUL HABIT.

MY BUSINESS IS NOT WHAT IT ONCE WAS.

THEY HAVEN'T THE TIME NOR INCLINATION FOR SWEETHEARTS, MUCH LESS WINDOW SHOPPING. THEY'RE ALWAYS IN A HURRY TO GET HOME.

MAY I INTRODUCE MYSELF? ABEL MARAH, IMPORTER OF RELIGIOUS ARTICLES.

I DON'T SHAKE THE HAND OF ANY STRANGER UNLESS IT'S CALLOUSED FROM HARD WORK.

YES, OF COURSE, I UNDERSTAND.

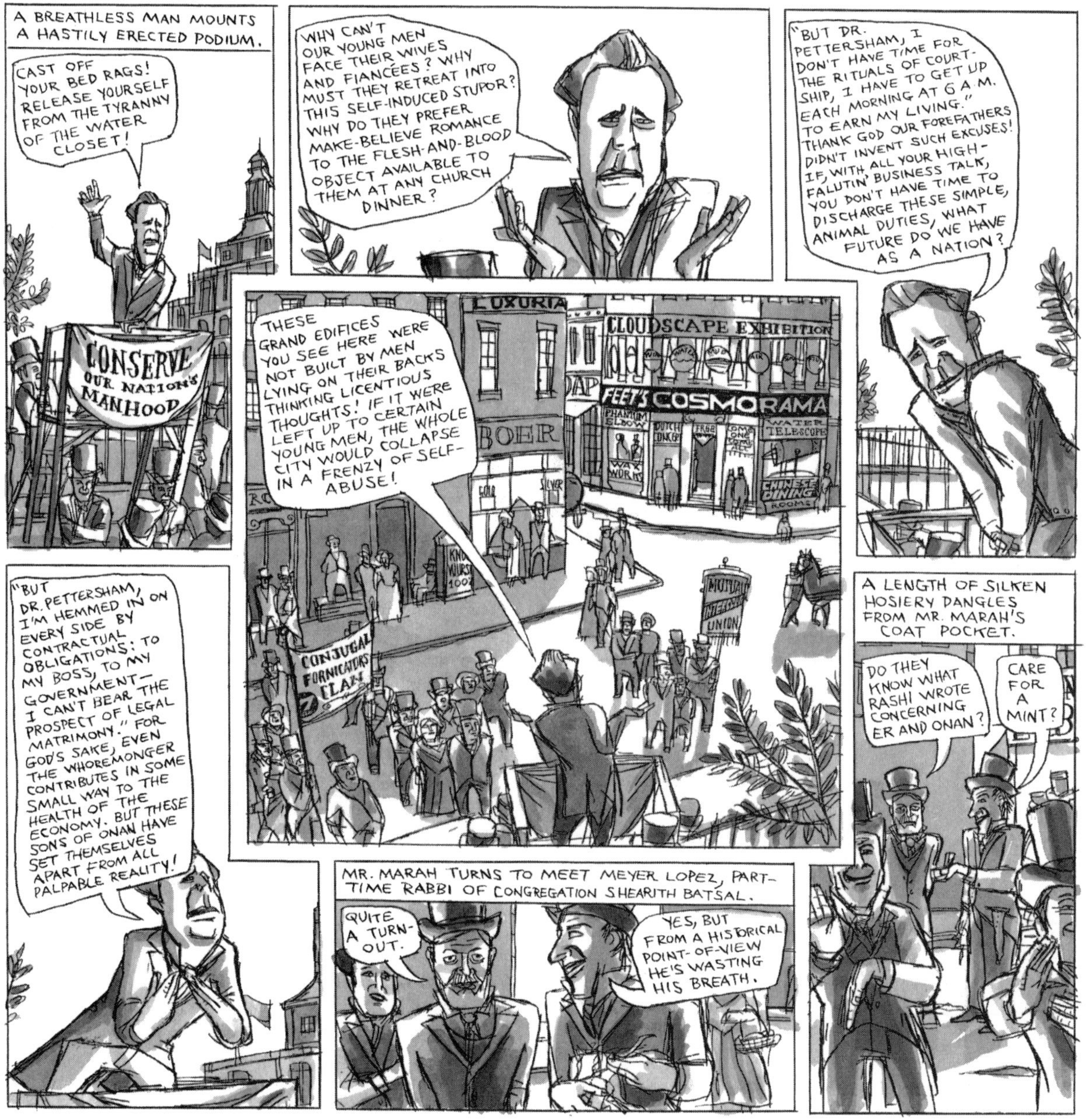
A BREATHLESS MAN MOUNTS A HASTILY ERECTED PODIUM.
CAST OFF YOUR BED RAGS! RELEASE YOURSELF FROM THE TYRANNY OF THE WATER CLOSET!
CONSERVE OUR NATION'S MANHOOD
WHY CAN'T OUR YOUNG MEN FACE THEIR WIVES AND FIANCÉES? WHY MUST THEY RETREAT INTO THIS SELF-INDUCED STUPOR? WHY DO THEY PREFER MAKE-BELIEVE ROMANCE TO THE FLESH-AND-BLOOD OBJECT AVAILABLE TO THEM AT ANY CHURCH DINNER?
"BUT DR. PETTERSHAM, I DON'T HAVE TIME FOR THE RITUALS OF COURTSHIP, I HAVE TO GET UP EACH MORNING AT 6 A.M. TO EARN MY LIVING." THANK GOD OUR FOREFATHERS DIDN'T INVENT SUCH EXCUSES! IF, WITH ALL YOUR HIGH-FALUTIN' BUSINESS TALK, YOU DON'T HAVE TIME TO DISCHARGE THESE SIMPLE, ANIMAL DUTIES, WHAT FUTURE DO WE HAVE AS A NATION?
LUXURIA
CLOUDSCAPE EXHIBITION
FEET'S COSMORAMA
BOER
CHINESE DINING ROOMS
THESE GRAND EDIFICES YOU SEE HERE WERE NOT BUILT BY MEN LYING ON THEIR BACKS THINKING LICENTIOUS THOUGHTS! IF IT WERE LEFT UP TO CERTAIN YOUNG MEN, THE WHOLE CITY WOULD COLLAPSE IN A FRENZY OF SELF-ABUSE!
"BUT DR. PETTERSHAM, I'M HEMMED IN ON EVERY SIDE BY CONTRACTUAL OBLIGATIONS: TO MY BOSS, TO MY GOVERNMENT— I CAN'T BEAR THE PROSPECT OF LEGAL MATRIMONY." FOR GOD'S SAKE, EVEN THE WHOREMONGER CONTRIBUTES IN SOME SMALL WAY TO THE HEALTH OF THE ECONOMY. BUT THESE SONS OF ONAN HAVE SET THEMSELVES APART FROM ALL PALPABLE REALITY!
MR. MARAH TURNS TO MEET MEYER LOPEZ, PART-TIME RABBI OF CONGREGATION SHEARITH BATSAL.
QUITE A TURN-OUT.
YES, BUT FROM A HISTORICAL POINT-OF-VIEW HE'S WASTING HIS BREATH.
A LENGTH OF SILKEN HOSIERY DANGLES FROM MR. MARAH'S COAT POCKET.
DO THEY KNOW WHAT RASHI WROTE CONCERNING ER AND ONAN?
CARE FOR A MINT?

MR. MARAH TURNS HIS BACK ON THE RALLY AND WANDERS HOME.

AN ENTERTAINING ORATION, BUT, IN FACT, MY SALES OF PHYLACTERIES, TSITSITHS AND EVEN MEZUZOTH ARE DWINDLING. DOES ANYONE ASK WHERE MY NEW CUSTOMERS ARE COMING FROM?

SHAUL JUVENAL IS A CONFIRMED BACHELOR; OTHERS ARE INVOLVED IN FRUITLESS OR UNCONSUMMATED MARRIAGES. NATHAN KISHON, HIMSELF A STRAPPING YOUNG MAN, LOST HIS WIFE TO A FALLING TREE AND NEVER REMARRIED.

ELIEZER YASCO MARRIED TWICE: A METHODIST AND THEN A FREE-MARKET SHAKER, AND MEANWHILE, ABRAHAM KURAL IS WHOLESALING WATERPROOF RUBBER CONDOMS AND DOING A BIG BUSINESS.

HE ABSENTMINDEDLY FINGERS THE SILKEN GARMENT IN HIS COAT POCKET.

AND THEN THESE ARTICLES ARE HANDED DOWN FROM FATHER TO SON, AND WHEN THE SON LOSES INTEREST, THE SAME ITEMS ARE SOLD BACK INTO AN EVER-SHRINKING MARKET.

TO PROVIDE FOR MY WIFE AND DAUGHTER I MUST DIVERSIFY. — TURN MY ATTENTION TOWARD A MORE LUCRATIVE BUSINESS.

THROUGH AN ADROIT JUGGLING OF ASSETS, MY BANK WILL BE ABLE TO ISSUE A DRAFT TO MR. LORGNETTE FOR SEVEN HUNDRED PAIRS OF FLESHINGS BEFORE OUR FIRST SALE OF BEAVER PELTS ACTUALLY TAKES PLACE.

MY CORELIGIONISTS HAVE DISSIPATED THEIR GENERATIVE ENERGIES IN THE PURSUIT OF BUSINESS. ANIMAL BREEDERS KNOW THAT A BULLOCK PUT OUT TO PASTURE WILL SIRE SIX TIMES THE NUMBER OF CALVES AS ONE KEPT IN HARNESS — MY HAND IS FORCED!

THIS CASTOREUM SHOULD BE BAKED INTO OUR PASSOVER MATZOS.

ABEL, COME TO BED.

AMERICAN HOTEL.

NEW YORK, SUNDAY, AUGUST 12, 1830

HOLMAN SOULPEAN

Bill of Fare—Businessman's Dinne[...]

Soup.

Turtle   Oarlock

Fish.

Poached Turbot, en cage.

Boiled.

Foreleg of Goat, Caper Sauce.   Pickled Lung.   Trotters.

Hill of Beef, with Andalusian Onion.   Assorted Tripes.

Entrees.

Bullock Heart, Stuffed with	Yanked Chicken on a Plate
Veal Forcemeat.	Deceased Mutton, a la
Underaged Chicken, with Egg.	Washington.
Calf of Lamb, in Titiano sauce.	Cornered Beef and Greens
Mystery Croquettes.	Mock Boar, in a Piquant
Stag Head, Dressed with	Sauce.
Brains.	

Relishes.

Galvanic Pickles   Berlin Picalli

Dessert

Tower of Babel Cake   Madonna Pudding   Fauntleroy Jelly

REFRAIN.

Whereas, it is admitted that the Practice of

ONANISM

IN PRIVATE HOUSES,

Is Engaged in on a Nightly Basis,
Its Effect is Underestimated.

Dr. Pettersham and The Mutual Intercourse Union, Hereby Stand and GIVE NOTICE that this practice be considered a form of TREASON, a crime punishable by DEATH.

Dated this 10th August, 1830,

DR. V. PETTERSHAM,

President and Acting Physician-in-Residence

G. VILLOTINAS, PRINTER AND SELLER OF GUMMED PAPERS, Queen St.

ENOCH LETUSHIM, A PALESTINIAN MESSENGER, WANDERS ALONG BROADWAY WITH A SMALL BAG OF SOIL FROM THE HOLY LAND.

HIS POCKETS ARE FILLED WITH DOCUMENTS TESTIFYING TO HIS AUTHENTICITY

I CAN'T MAKE THIS OUT

AND YET HE MEETS JEWS IN NEW YORK CITY WHO DOUBT HIS SINCERITY.

HE MAY BE ONE OF THOSE PROFESSIONAL IMPOSTORS

WHY MUST HE CARRY THEIR DONATIONS BACK TO JERUSALEM PERSONALLY?

WHY NOT SEND THE MONIES TO PALESTINE VIA THE AUTHORITIES IN LONDON?

YOU SEEM TO BE AN ABLE-BODIED MAN

ARE THERE STILL JEWS IN THIS CITY WHO CARE TO BE BURIED ALONG WITH SOIL FROM THE HOLY LAND?

IN DEATH, THEY SAY, ALL DISTINCTIONS WHICH EXISTED IN LIFE SHOULD BE REMOVED,

AMERICAN HOTEL

THE RICH AND POOR SHOULD MINGLE IN THEIR ETERNAL REST.

IN THE EVENING, HE ANOINTS HIMSELF WITH OILS AND PERFUME.

ALMOST ONE THOUSAND JEWS IN THIS CITY ALONE

INTOXICATED BY THE SMELL OF BERGAMOT AND MYRRH EMANATING FROM HIS OWN BODY, ENOCH LETUSHIM, THE PALESTINIAN MESSENGER, RETURNS TO THE HOTEL LOBBY

IN SOME CASES I'VE BEEN COMPLETELY MISTAKEN. THEY ARE JEWS, BUT BORN AND EDUCATED IN THIS COUNTRY.

AND STANDS NEAR THE FRONT DOOR AS THOUGH WAITING FOR SOMEONE.

I MUST WAIT FOR THEM TO GIVE ME A SMILE OF RECOGNITION

HE OVERHEARS THE DETAILS OF ONE MAN'S COMMERCIAL MACHINATIONS.

WITH THE PROFITS FROM A SCYTHE FACTORY IN LOWELL, I BOUGHT SIX ICE HOUSES ON THE HUDSON. THIS IN TURN ALLOWED ME TO ACQUIRE AN INTEREST IN THE...

HE TRIES TO UNDERSTAND THE SECRET DESIGN OF AMERICAN WOMEN'S CLOTHING.

A PEDDLER OFFERS OLD BOTTLES OF LAKE ERIE WATER.

JOIN THE CELEBRATION!

ACROSS THE STREET, HE SEES ANOTHER PALESTINIAN MESSENGER EMPTY A SACK OF DIRT INTO THE GUTTER.

ONE ELEGANTLY DRESSED MAN WIPES HIS NOSE ON A HANDKERCHIEF EMBROIDERED WITH WHAT APPEAR TO BE KABBALISTIC DESIGNS.

MAYBE A JEW

A YOUNG MAN READS ALOUD FROM THE LATEST EDITION OF "NILES' REGISTER."

HERE, LISTEN TO THIS

AND ENOCH LETUSHIM FEELS AN UNSEASONABLE CHILL BENEATH HIS KAFTAN.

"THERE IS A REPORT THAT THE ROTHSCHILDS HAVE PURCHASED JERUSALEM."

"WE SEE NOTHING IMPROBALE THAT, IN THE PECUNIARY DISTRESS OF THE SULTAN, HE SHOULD SELL SOME PART OF HIS DOMINIONS TO PRESERVE THE REST..."

I'VE HEARD THESE RUMORS BEFORE

"OR THAT THE ROTHSCHILDS SHOULD PURCHASE THE ANCIENT CAPITAL OF THEIR NATION..."

OR THAT MEN SHOULD STILL BE TRYING TO SELL LAKE ERIE WATER!

PEOPLE IN THIS COUNTRY WANT MORE THAN FRESH WATER WITH THEIR MEALS

ERIE WATER!

THEY WANT CARBONATED WATER...SODA WATER! SOMETHING WITH A KICK, SOMETHING TO AID DIGESTION!

IT'S AN INVENTION OF THE GENIUS PRIESTLEY... WAITING SIXTY YEARS TO BE EXPLOITED ON A GRAND SCALE.

I DRANK A SODA WATER IN LONDON.

MY DREAM IS THE CARBONATION OF LAKE ERIE! IT'S SIMPLE... A STEADY SUPPLY OF GAS CAN BE PRODUCED BY TREATING THE LAKE'S NATURAL CHALK DEPOSITS WITH SULPHURIC ACID

HE WIPES HIS NOSE AGAIN ON THE HANDKERCHIEF EMBROIDERED WITH KABBALISTIC SYMBOLS.

I ESTIMATE A MILLION BOTTLES A YEAR.

YES, YES BROTHER, ALL I LACK IS SUFFICIENT CAPITAL.

"THEY ARE WEALTHY BEYOND THE DESIRE, PERHAPS, EVEN OF AVARICE"

THE MAN WHO DREAMS OF CARBONATING LAKE ERIE CRIES ON ENOCH LETUSHIM'S SHOULDER.

YES, YES, BROTHER. ALL I LACK IS SUFFICIENT CAPITAL

AMERICAN HOTEL

ON TUESDAY EVENINGS, THEY SERVE A BULLOCK'S HEART STUFFED WITH VEAL FORCEMEAT.

AND THIS, YOU SEE, IS ONE OF THE FEW HOTELS ON BROADWAY EQUIPPED WITH A SODA WATER FOUNTAIN.

I STAND HERE IN THE LOBBY WAITING FOR WEALTHY MEN TO LEAVE THE DINING ROOM.

SOME STROLL OUT WITH A GLASS OF SODA WATER IN THEIR HAND! WHAT BETTER OPPORTUNITY TO APPROACH A POTENTIAL... AH!

GREPTZ

GOOD EVENING. ENJOYING YOUR SODA WATER? AIDS THE DIGESTION, DOESN'T IT?

HAVE WE MET BEFORE?

NO, NOT EXACTLY, BUT I SEE THAT YOU'RE A MAN WHO APPRECIATES A GOOD, COLD GLASS OF SODA WATER AND I THEREFORE BELIEVE THAT YOU'LL ALSO APPRECIATE A DREAM I HAD SEVERAL MONTHS AGO. A DREAM I HOPE TO REALIZE WITHIN MY LIFETIME. A DREAM THAT MANY OTHERS HAVE HAD, BUT FORGOT UPON WAKING TO THE HAR—

GOOD EVENING.

HE USES A HANDKERCHIEF EMBROIDERED WITH KABBALISTIC SYMBOLS TO WIPE THE SPITTLE FROM THE CORNER OF HIS MOUTH.

THE NAME IS ORIOLE, LIKE THE GOLDEN BIRD, AND A GOOD EVENING TO YOU AS WELL!

MR. MARAH ENTERTAINS A POTENTIAL CUSTOMER IN THE DINING ROOM OF THE AMERICAN HOTEL ON BROADWAY.

YOU SAY THE MAJORITY OF THESE PELTS ARE OF YOUNG TO MIDDLE-AGED BEAVERS?

THIS BULLOCK'S HEART HAS DONE ME IN

YES, YES. MANY FINE CUBS... A SODA WATER, PLEASE

I'LL NOTIFY MY CUSTOMERS IN LONDON, AND IF THEY'RE INTERESTED...

AH! MY LIFE HAS BEEN SAVED

WE CAN DISCUSS THE PARTICULARS OF DELIVERY AT THAT TIME.

HERE'S A LIKELY PROSPECT

GREPTZ

GOOD EVENING. ENJOYING YOUR SODA WATER? AIDS THE DIGESTION, DOESN'T IT?

A WONDER BEVERAGE! SHOULD BE PIPED INTO EVERY AMERICAN HOME!

AND CAN YOU IMAGINE THE PROFITS OF SUCH AN ENTERPRISE CONDUCTED ON A VAST SCALE?

MY NAME IS FRANCIS ORIOLE, AND I REPRESENT THE LAKE ERIE SODA WATER COMPANY. IN THE COMING YEAR, WE INTEND TO CARBONATE LAKE ERIE AND LAY A HIGH-PRESSURE PIPE LINE DIRECTLY TO NEW YORK CITY.

IN A STRANGE HOTEL LOBBY, FAR FROM PALESTINE, ENOCH LETUSHIM SUDDENLY FEELS AT HOME.

OF COURSE, SUCH AN UNDERTAKING WILL REQUIRE A SUBSTANTIAL CAPITAL INVESTMENT.

WAITER, PLEASE. A ROUND OF SODA WATERS

[46]

FROM THE LOBBY OF THE AMERICAN HOTEL, AT DINNER TIME, ENOCH LETUSHIM OBSERVES A STREAM OF BUSINESSMEN AND WOMEN MOVING AT A HEALTHY PACE ALONG BROADWAY, THEIR EYES DIRECTED TOWARD THE FUTURE.

A REFRESHING CHANGE FROM THE CROOKED STREETS OF JERUSALEM AND ITS ENVIRONS

IT HAPPENED RIGHT HERE...

WHERE UNSCRUPULOUS GUIDES LIE IN WAIT FOR CREDULOUS PILGRIMS WHO ARE EAGER TO LEARN

TWO THOUSAND YEARS AGO!

THE HISTORICAL AND RELIGIOUS SIGNIFICANCE OF THE GROUND UPON WHICH THEY HAPPEN TO BE STANDING AT THAT MOMENT.

HERE WE HAVE THE CHAPEL OF ADAM, WHERE IT IS SAID THE HEAD OF THE FIRST MAN WAS BURIED BY SHEM, THE SON OF NOAH, AFTER THE DELUGE.

THIS IS THE VERY PLACE IN WHICH THE PROPHET JEREMIAH GAVE UTTERANCE TO HIS SORROW IN "THE LAMENTATIONS."

"MY BELOVED IS UNTO ME AS A CLUSTER OF CAMPHIRE IN THE VINEYARDS OF EN-GEDI." (SONG OF SOLOMON, i, 14.)

ALL THESE PLACES ARE DESCRIBED AS THE TRUE AND GENUINE PLACES WHERE THE EVENTS ACTUALLY TOOK PLACE IN THE TIMES REFERRED TO

THIS IS THE CAVE OF ADULLAM IN WHICH DAVID HID HIMSELF FROM THE PERSECUTION OF SAUL.

THOUGH IT IS WELL KNOWN THAT EVEN JERUSALEM ITSELF DOES NOT STAND ON THE SAME SPOT OF GROUND WHICH IT OCCUPIED IN THE TIME OF CHRIST.[1]

WHERE ISAIAH WAS SAWN ASUNDER IN THE TRUNK OF A TREE

[1] Châteaubriand, "L'Intinéraire de Paris à Jérusalem et de Jérusalem à Paris" (1811)

[47]

OUT OF CURIOSITY, ENOCH LETUSHIM QUESTIONS A HOTEL PORTER.

IS THERE ANY HISTORY ASSOCIATED WITH THIS CORNER OF BROADWAY? WHAT STOOD HERE BEFORE THE HOTEL?

BEFORE THIS BUILDING, THERE STOOD ON THIS SITE FOR MANY YEARS THE ORIGINAL AMERICAN HOTEL—

A MODEST EDIFICE KNOWN FOR ITS PROXIMITY TO THE PARK THEATRE AND FOR ITS OYSTER BAR.

BEFORE THAT, IT WAS FOR A SHORT PERIOD OF TIME AN OPEN PLACE WHERE STRAY DOGS WERE ROUNDED UP TO BE KILLED.

AND BEFORE THAT, IT WAS THE FRONT GARDEN OF A HOUSE BELONGING TO A DUTCH FEATHER DYER

AND BEFORE THAT, IT WAS A ROPEWALK ON THE OUTSKIRTS OF THE CITY

AND BEFORE THAT... YOU'LL HAVE TO ASK AN INDIAN.

ENOCH LETUSHIM FOLLOWS THE STRANGER INTO THE HOTEL'S PUBLIC BAR.

AN ABORIGINAL MAN, HERE, IN THE LOBBY! I'LL OFFER HIM A DRINK.

TELL ME, DO YOUR PEOPLE HAVE ANY HISTORY ASSOCIATED WITH THIS CORNER OF BROADWAY?

I'VE BEEN HERE ONLY A FEW DAYS. I COME FROM BUFFALO.

SUCCESS! SUCCESS! FRIDAY NIGHT'S PERFORMANCE IS COMPLETELY SOLD-OUT!

EXCUSE ME.

THE MANAGEMENT OF HIRAM'S MUSEUM HAS EXTENDED OUR ENGAGEMENT TO THE END OF THE MONTH.

I'VE HIRED A RELIABLE GROUP OF MINYAN-MEN AND SET UP A BEAUTIFUL LITTLE SYNAGOGUE RIGHT ON THE STAGE!

THEY'RE PLASTERING THE CITY WITH POSTERS. THE PUBLIC'S CURIOSITY HAS BEEN WHIPPED TO A FROTH!

A RECITATION

In Perfect Hebrew! BY A RARE, LIVING MEMBER of ONE OF THE 10 LOST TRIBES OF ISRAEL! RESCUED FROM THE WILDS OF UPPER NEW YORK STATE.

WELCOMING THE SABBATH

PSALMS 95-99 AND OTHER HYMNS!

FRIDAY NIGHT

HIRAM'S MUSEUM BROADWAY

COME, HAVE A DRINK. LET'S GO OVER THE HYMN, "LECHON DODI," ONE MORE TIME.

לְכָה דוֹדִי לִקְרַאת
בַּלָה · פְּנֵי שַׁבָּת
נְקַבְּלָה ...

[49]

ISAAC AZARAEL WAS NOW CERTAIN THAT THE NAKED INDIAN HE SAW SLEEPING IN THE STREET, EACH NIGHT, ACROSS FROM THE GIBRALTAR HOTEL

I HAVE MY OWN TROUBLES... BUT HOW CAN I IGNORE THIS?

WAS, IN FACT, A JEW — SOME REMNANT OF A LOST TRIBE OF ISRAEL.

MY SHIP MAY OR MAY NOT BE LOST AT SEA, BUT THIS MAN'S PLIGHT IS OBVIOUS!

I SAW HIM, DURING THE DAY, EXAMINING MEAT IN THE WINDOW OF A KOSHER BUTCHER.

I SAW HIM DEALING WITH A WELL-KNOWN IMPORTER OF PHYLACTERIES.

I SAW HIM READING THE NOTICES POSTED OUTSIDE OF SHEARITH BATSAL.

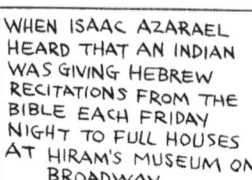

WHEN ISAAC AZARAEL HEARD THAT AN INDIAN WAS GIVING HEBREW RECITATIONS FROM THE BIBLE EACH FRIDAY NIGHT TO FULL HOUSES AT HIRAM'S MUSEUM ON BROADWAY...

HIS NAME IS ELIM-MIN-NOPEE. HE LIVED, UNTIL NOW, IN THE WILDS OF UPPER NEW YORK STATE YET KNOWS THE PSALMS BY HEART, IN HEBREW!

HE WAS COMPELLED TO BRING HIS DISCOVERY TO THE ATTENTION OF THE SYNAGOGUE'S MUTUAL AID SOCIETY.

YOU CAN SEE WITH YOUR OWN EYES THAT HE'S LEFT TO SLEEP IN THE STREET AT NIGHT LIKE A DOG!

ARE YOU SURE IT'S THE SAME MAN?

QUIET. YOU'LL WAKE HIM.

A LETTER WAS SENT BY THE SECRETARY OF THE MUTUAL AID SOCIETY WELCOMING ELIM-MIN-NOPEE TO NEW YORK CITY ON BEHALF OF CONGREGATION SHEARITH BATSAL

TO HIRAM'S MUSEUM ON BROADWAY.

AND INCIDENTALLY INQUIRING AS TO SUITABILITY AND COMFORT OF HIS ACCOMODATIONS.

EVERY TOWN HAS ITS MEDDLESOME BUSYBODIES.

HERSHEL GOULBAT, HIS MANAGER, WROTE BACK THE SAME AFTERNOON, THANKING THEM ON BEHALF OF ELIM-MIN-NOPEE

TO SHEARITH BATSAL SYNAGOGUE

AND ASSURING THEM THAT A MAN RAISED IN THE WILDS OF UPPER NEW YORK STATE HAD QUICKLY BECOME ACCUSTOMED TO HIS LUXURIOUS ROOM IN THE AMERICAN HOTEL ON BROADWAY. FOUR PASSES FOR THAT EVENING'S PERFORMANCE WERE INCLUDED WITH THE LETTER.

HE'S LYING! WE MUST CONFRONT HIM WITH THE FACTS!

LATER THAT SAME AFTERNOON, A LETTER WAS DRAFTED BY THE SECRETARY OF THE MUTUAL AID SOCIETY THANKING MR. GOULBAT FOR CONVEYING THEIR MESSAGE TO ELIM-MIN-NOPEE, AND HOPING THAT HE WAS ENJOYING THE FRUITS OF CIVILIZATION AS OFFERED TO ALL MEN IN THIS GREAT CITY.

TO THE AMERICAN HOTEL ON BROADWAY.

A POSTSCRIPT TO THE LETTER THANKED MR. GOULBAT FOR THE FREE PASSES AND INCIDENTALLY INQUIRED AS TO WHETHER HE WAS AWARE OF ANOTHER JEW, ALSO RAISED BY AN ABORIGINAL TRIBE, WHO SLEPT EACH NIGHT IN THE STREET ACROSS FROM THE GIBRALTAR HOTEL.

THE BASTARDS! THEY'RE THREATENING TO PRESENT A RIVAL ATTRACTION! TO CASH IN ON OUR SUCCESS. NEXT, THEY'LL ASK FOR A CUT OF MY PROFITS! THE SWINE!

MR. GOULBAT WROTE BACK, WITHIN THE HOUR, TO SAY THAT HE WAS SURPRISED TO LEARN OF THE PRESENCE IN THE CITY OF ANOTHER LIVING MEMBER OF ONE OF THE LOST TRIBES OF ISRAEL. TO THE BEST OF HIS KNOWLEDGE, ELIM-MIN-NOPEE WAS THE ONLY GENUINE, HEBREW-SPEAKING INDIAN CURRENTLY IN TOWN.

WE'LL ATTEND TONIGHT'S PERFORMANCE AND SEE FOR OURSELVES.

HE THANKED THE SECRETARY FOR BRINGING THIS INTERESTING PIECE OF INFORMATION TO HIS ATTENTION, AND HOPED THAT IT WOULD NOT, IN ANY WAY, MAR THE SECRETARY'S ENJOYMENT OF THE SHOW AT HIRAM'S MUSEUM.

I'LL BE THERE TONIGHT ACROSS FROM THE GIBRALTAR HOTEL AND SEE WHO PUT THEM UP TO THIS!

IN THE LOBBY OF HIRAM'S MUSEUM, ISAAC AZARAEL STOPS TO GAZE AT A CLOD OF EARTH PURPORTEDLY TAKEN FROM THE SITE OF THE GARDEN OF EDEN IN MESOPOTAMIA.

THE SHOW'S STARTING.

WELCOMING THE SABBATH

ARE YOU CERTAIN IT'S THE SAME MAN?

THEY USE TREMENDOUS QUANTITIES OF STAGE MAKE-UP.

HE SEEMS BROADER IN THE FACE TO ME.

AS THE SHOW PROGRESSES, ISAAC AZARAEL REALIZES THAT HE HAS MADE A TERRIBLE MISTAKE.

YOU'RE RIGHT. THIS MAN IS BROADER IN THE FACE.

לכה דודי

LATE THAT NIGHT, HERSHEL GOULBAT APPROACHES THE GIBRALTAR HOTEL WITH A STICK IN HIS HAND.

PEOPLE EXPECT TO PROFIT FROM MY HARD LABOR.

HERE! WHAT'S THIS!? ANOTHER WOULD-BE ABORIGINAL JEW!

SHALL I KILL HIM IN HIS SLEEP OR JUST DISFIGURE HIM FOR LIFE?

QUIET. YOU'LL WAKE HIM.

LIKE OTHER YOUNG MEN WHOSE DAYS ARE SPENT IN WILD COMMERCIAL SPECULATION, FRANCIS ORIOLE, PRESIDENT OF THE LAKE ERIE SODA WATER COMPANY, WANDERS THE STREET AT NIGHT, UNABLE TO SLEEP.

HE STOPS FOR A MOMENT TO LISTEN TO THE DISTANT SOUND OF A WHIPPING...

A DOG OR RUNAWAY SLAVE?

FITTT... AY! FITTT... AY! AY!

AND IS REMINDED OF THE TERRIBLE WORK WHICH LIES BEFORE HIM.

TO TAME A VAST INLAND SEA, ALONG WITH ALL THE MEN AND CREATURES WHO LIVE ON ITS SHORE...

THE INDIANS WHO HAVE LITTLE REGARD FOR SODA WATER

THE FEW NORTH AMERICAN DISCIPLES OF COMTE DE SAINT-SIMON WHO HAIL SODA WATER AS THE SACRAMENTAL BEVERAGE OF THEIR NEW RELIGION OF THE FLESH.

THE FUR TRADERS WHO BLAME CARBONATION FOR THE BEAVER'S FLAGGING DESIRE TO PROCREATE.

AND THE AQUATIC ANIMALS WHOSE PRIMITIVE LUNGS CANNOT TOLERATE SUCH HIGHLY GASEOUS WATER.

FROM THE SOUND OF A FELLOW CREATURE BEING MERCILESSLY FLOGGED IN THE STREET, HE DERIVES A FEELING OF CALM REASSURANCE.

YES, EVEN THESE OBSTACLES CAN BE OVERCOME.

FFFIT. AY! AY! FFFFIT AY! AY!

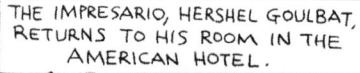
THE IMPRESARIO, HERSHEL GOULBAT, RETURNS TO HIS ROOM IN THE AMERICAN HOTEL.

WHAT HAPPENED TO YOUR FACE?

I APPROACHED THE GIBRALTAR HOTEL WITH A STICK IN MY HAND, DETERMINED TO SCARE OFF OUR WOULD-BE COMPETITORS.

ACROSS THE WAY, ON A PATCH OF GRASS, I SAW A FIGURE SLEEPING, WRAPPED IN A BLANKET, AS YOUR PEOPLE ARE WONT TO DO.

IN THE MOONLIGHT, I COULD MAKE OUT THE FEATURES OF A DEGENERATE IROQUOIS BRAVE... POSSIBLY A HALF-BREED.

I HESITATED FOR A MOMENT ... SHOULD I KILL HIM IN HIS SLEEP OR JUST DISFIGURE HIM FOR LIFE AND THUS PUT AN END TO HIS FUTURE ON THE STAGE?

IN THAT MOMENT OF HESITATION, I WAS SET UPON BY AN ENRAGED BRUTE. I NOTED THAT HIS JACKET WAS TASTE-LESSLY DECORATED WITH MOTHER-OF-PEARL BUTTONS.

IN THE NAME OF THE MUTUAL AID SOCIETY OF SHEARITH BATSAL, HE THREW ME TO THE GROUND AND THEN, AS THOUGH I WERE AN OLD ACQUAINTANCE OF HIS, THRASHED ME WITH MY OWN STICK!

HIS ONLY CONCERN WAS THAT WE NOT WAKE THE SLEEPING INDIAN.

QUIET. QUIET. YOU'LL WAKE HIM.

AY! AY!

TO SAVE MY LIFE, I WENT SO FAR AS TO OFFER HIM A TEN PERCENT CUT OF OUR PROFITS... BUT IT WAS TO NO AVAIL.

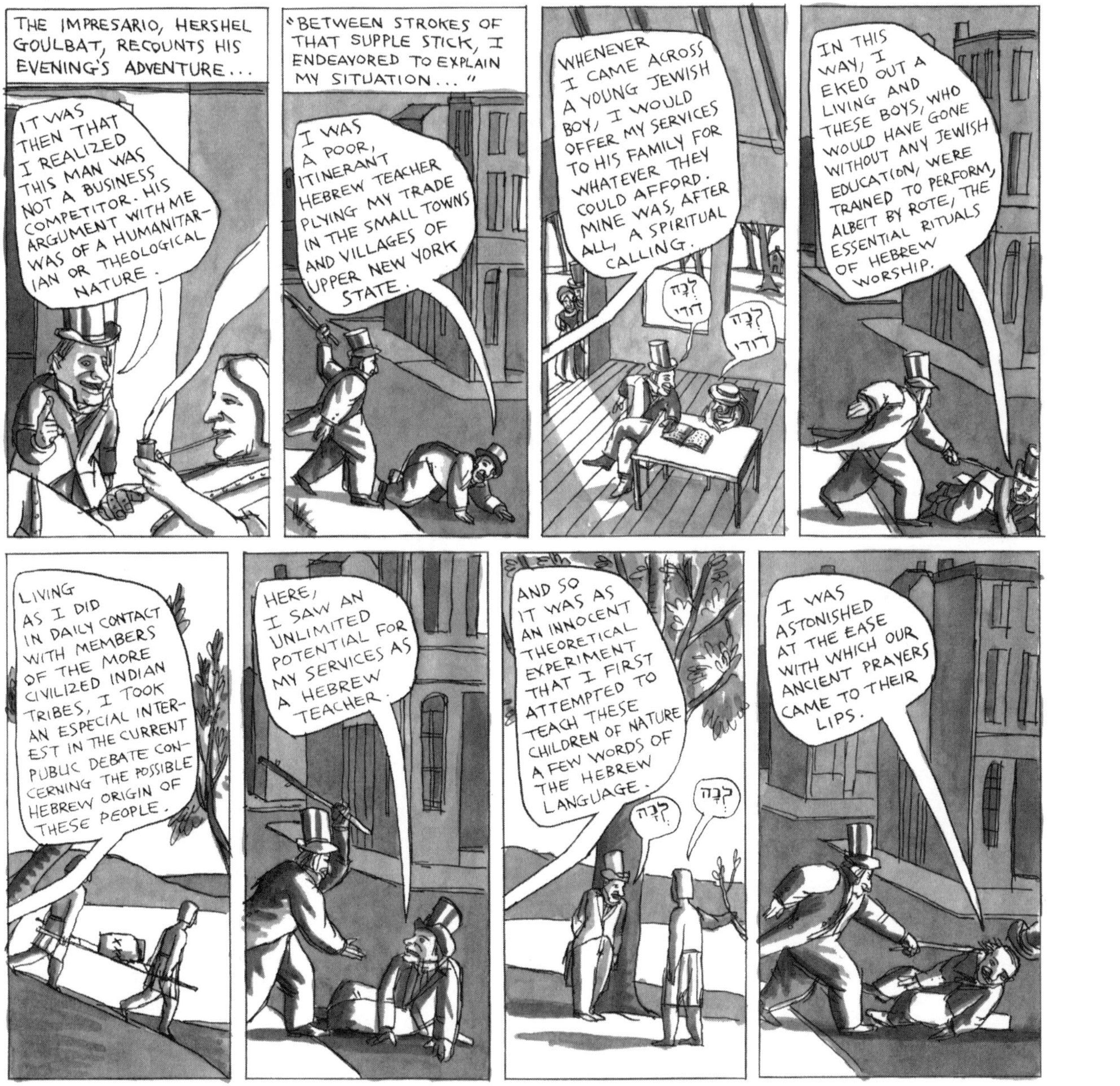
THE IMPRESARIO, HERSHEL GOULBAT, RECOUNTS HIS EVENING'S ADVENTURE...
IT WAS THEN THAT I REALIZED THIS MAN WAS NOT A BUSINESS COMPETITOR. HIS ARGUMENT WITH ME WAS OF A HUMANITARIAN OR THEOLOGICAL NATURE.
"BETWEEN STROKES OF THAT SUPPLE STICK, I ENDEAVORED TO EXPLAIN MY SITUATION..."
I WAS A POOR, ITINERANT HEBREW TEACHER PLYING MY TRADE IN THE SMALL TOWNS AND VILLAGES OF UPPER NEW YORK STATE.
WHENEVER I CAME ACROSS A YOUNG JEWISH BOY, I WOULD OFFER MY SERVICES TO HIS FAMILY FOR WHATEVER THEY COULD AFFORD. MINE WAS, AFTER ALL, A SPIRITUAL CALLING.
לְכָה דודי
לְכָה דודי
IN THIS WAY, I EKED OUT A LIVING AND THESE BOYS, WHO WOULD HAVE GONE WITHOUT ANY JEWISH EDUCATION, WERE TRAINED TO PERFORM, ALBEIT BY ROTE, THE ESSENTIAL RITUALS OF HEBREW WORSHIP.
LIVING AS I DID IN DAILY CONTACT WITH MEMBERS OF THE MORE CIVILIZED INDIAN TRIBES, I TOOK AN ESPECIAL INTEREST IN THE CURRENT PUBLIC DEBATE CONCERNING THE POSSIBLE HEBREW ORIGIN OF THESE PEOPLE.
HERE, I SAW AN UNLIMITED POTENTIAL FOR MY SERVICES AS A HEBREW TEACHER.
AND SO IT WAS AS AN INNOCENT THEORETICAL EXPERIMENT THAT I FIRST ATTEMPTED TO TEACH THESE CHILDREN OF NATURE A FEW WORDS OF THE HEBREW LANGUAGE.
לְכָה
לְכָה
I WAS ASTONISHED AT THE EASE WITH WHICH OUR ANCIENT PRAYERS CAME TO THEIR LIPS.

AT LAST, I WAS ABLE TO CONVINCE HIM THAT HE HAD, WITH THE BEST OF IN-TENTIONS, UNKNOW-INGLY WALKED INTO THE MIDST OF A DISPUTE AMONG INCOMPLETELY CIVILIZED YESHIVA BOYS.

YOUR DESIRE TO PREVENT THE COMMISSION OF A CARDINAL SIN IS TO BE COMMENDED, BUT IN THIS CASE THERE'S BEEN A SIMPLE MISAPPRE-HENSION OF THE FACTS.

I CAME HERE TONIGHT ON A DISCIPLINARY MISSION. IN MY CAREER AS A HEBREW TEACHER I'VE DISCOVERED THAT A STICK IS THE BEST WAY TO CURB THE JEALOUS RIVALRY WHICH SOMETIMES DEVELOPS AMONGST YOUNG MEN.

MY TALK OF KILLING AND MAIMING WAS OF A FIGURATIVE NATURE... MERE SYMBOLIC EXAGGERA-TION. THESE INDIAN BOYS ARE MY PUPILS, MY SOURCE OF PRIDE AND INCOME.

I TOLD HIM THAT THE PROCEEDS FROM MY SHOW AT HIRAM'S MUSEUM WERE BEING USED TO ESTABLISH A GREAT YESHIVA IN THE WILDS OF UPPER NEW YORK STATE.

FOR I BELIEVE THAT UNTIL IT IS PROVEN OTHERWISE, WE MUST ACCEPT THESE CHILDREN OF NATURE AS FELLOW JEWS WHO HAVE TEMPORARILY LOST THEIR WAY IN THE NEW WORLD...

AND THAT IT IS OUR RESPONSIBILITY TO MAKE AVAILABLE TO THEM THE TEACHINGS OF ABRAHAM AND MOSES!

HE APOLOGIZED FOR HIS MISTAKE AND OFFERED TO MAKE A SMALL CONTRIBUTION TOWARD THE BUILDING OF THE YESHIVA I HAD INVENTED.

AT AN EVENING MEETING OF THE SHEARITH BATSAL MUTUAL AID SOCIETY...

LET US THANK MR. AZARAEL FOR BRINGING THIS SITUATION TO OUR ATTENTION. THERE IS, HOWEVER, NO MYSTERY. THE FELLOW SLEEPING IN THE STREET ACROSS FROM THE GIBRALTAR HOTEL IS NOT AN INDIAN, HE IS NATHAN KISHON, THE SHOYKHET FROM QUEEN STREET. — I RECOGNIZED HIM INSTANTLY. HE WAS INVOLVED, YOU MAY REMEMBER, IN A CONFUSION OVER BEEF TONGUES SEVERAL YEARS AGO.

HE WAS ONE OF THE FEW MEMBERS OF OUR CONGREGATION TO FOLLOW MORDECAI NOAH TO GRAND ISLAND, WHERE HE WAS FOR THE PAST FIVE YEARS IS NOT OUR CONCERN, BUT THAT HE'S NOW RETURNED AND SLEEPS IN THE STREET AND GOES ABOUT DRAPED IN A BEDSHEET SHOULD TROUBLE US DEEPLY. IT REFLECTS POORLY ON THE JEWISH COMMUNITY.

THIS IS NOT A CASE OF FINANCIAL HARDSHIP. KISHON HAS APPARENTLY HAD SOME SUCCESS IN BUSINESS. THE BELLBOY AT THE GIBRALTAR HOTEL TELLS ME THAT KISHON HAS PAID FOR HIS ROOM TWO MONTHS IN ADVANCE AND HAS HAD BUSINESS DEALINGS THERE WITH MR. ABEL MARAH.

WHAT BEGAN AS A MINOR LAPSE IN THE FULFILLMENT OF A JEWISH RITUAL LAW HAS DEEPENED, OVER TIME, INTO A COMPLETE REJECTION OF SOCIETY AND ITS WAYS. THE GOVERNING BOARD OF THIS SYNAGOGUE MAY HAVE BEEN TOO HARSH IN ITS JUDGEMENT AT THAT TIME. AND NOW WE MUST DEAL WITH THE SAD RESULTS.

PERHAPS HE'S TAKEN UP WITH A GROUP OF ESSENES. MY NIECE WON'T EAT MEAT AND WEARS ONLY WHITE DRESSES.

THE STREETS OF THIS CITY ARE FILLED WITH ECCENTRICS: DORMAT GISSEN, THE HERMIT OF CLIFF STREET, VILLY JANTZ, THE BOY WHO LIVES IN THE FLOWER MARKET. LET THESE PEOPLE LIVE OUT THEIR LIVES AS PARIAHS ON THE FRINGES OF SOCIETY — THEY WERE NOT ONCE MEMBERS OF OUR CONGREGATION.

SHOULD KISHON BE ARRESTED AS A COMMON VAGRANT, WE ARE ALL IMPLICATED. PEOPLE WILL TALK: "WHAT SORT OF A RELIGION DRIVES A MAN TO SUCH ABERRANT BEHAVIOR? MAYBE THERE IS SOME TRUTH TO THOSE OUTLANDISH LEGENDS CONCERNING THE JEWS?" WHO HAS THE TIME OR ENERGY TO COMPOSE A FORMAL REFUTATION OF THESE CHARGES, MUCH LESS PUBLISH AND DISTRIBUTE SUCH A DOCUMENT?

WOULDN'T IT BE FAR EASIER TO OFFER KISHON A NEW SUIT OF CLOTHES, FIND HIM A WIFE AND WELCOME HIM BACK INTO THE FOLD? AFTER ALL, HE IS AN EXPERIENCED BUTCHER.

YES, YES, THERE'S THE MINIS WIDOW, THE SECOR WIDOW, THE SIRACHT WIDOW: ALL BEAUTIFUL YOUNG WOMEN WHOSE HUSBANDS LOST THEIR LIVES IN THE PURSUIT OF BUSINESS.

I DONATE ONE WOOLEN DRESS SUIT, MADE TO ORDER.

AND I INVITE YOU ALL TO A DINNER PARTY AT MY HOME ON THURSDAY NIGHT IN HONOR OF NATHAN KISHON!

DURING A CHANCE ENCOUNTER IN A PUBLIC DINING ROOM, THE ACTOR MAYNARD DAIZY CONFIDES IN SAMSON GERGEL, THE SCENIC DECORATOR OF THE NEW WORLD THEATER.

IF I AM TO HAVE EVEN A MODICUM OF SUCCESS IN MY UPCOMING ROLE AS MAJOR HAM IN "THE JEW OF NEW YORK," I MUST GIVE THE PUBLIC SOMETHING NEW AND FASCINATING...

THE DIALOGUE ITSELF IS DEVOID OF HUMOR. WAITER! A BOWL OF TURTLE SOUP FOR MY FRIEND!

THE OLD STAGE CHARACTERIZATIONS NO LONGER RING TRUE IN THE FRESH AIR OF OUR YOUNG REPUBLIC.

YOU'RE RIGHT! YOU'RE RIGHT! I'VE HAD NO MORE ACQUAINTANCE WITH THE JEW, AS HE EXISTS IN THE FLESH, THAN WITH AN ESQUIMAU OR A MONGOLIAN SHEPHERD OR A...

AND YET I AM EXPECTED TO BRING A HUMOROUS INSIGHT TO HIS PREDICAMENT IN THE NEW WORLD.

PERHAPS I COULD INTRODUCE YOU TO A FEW OF MY FRIENDS... PERHAPS YOU COULD ATTEND A SERVICE AT MY SYNAGOGUE...

THE CENTURIES OF ISOLATION IN THE GHETTOS OF EUROPE ARE BEHIND YOU!

YES, MORE OR LESS.

THE SOCIAL OSTRACISM FROM THE MAINSTREAM OF CULTURE IS AT AN END!

THIS IS A RICH BROTH...

THE LIFE OF CONSTANT FEAR FROM PERSECUTION IS, IN THIS HEALTHY CLIMATE, THE MERE STUFF OF HISTORICAL ANECDOTE!

CONSIDERING THAT I'VE ALREADY HAD A SUBSTANTIAL MIDDAY MEAL.

I WANT TO MEET THE JEW OF NEW YORK AS HE ACTUALLY LIVES AND BREATHES!

WAITER... A SODA WATER, PLEASE.

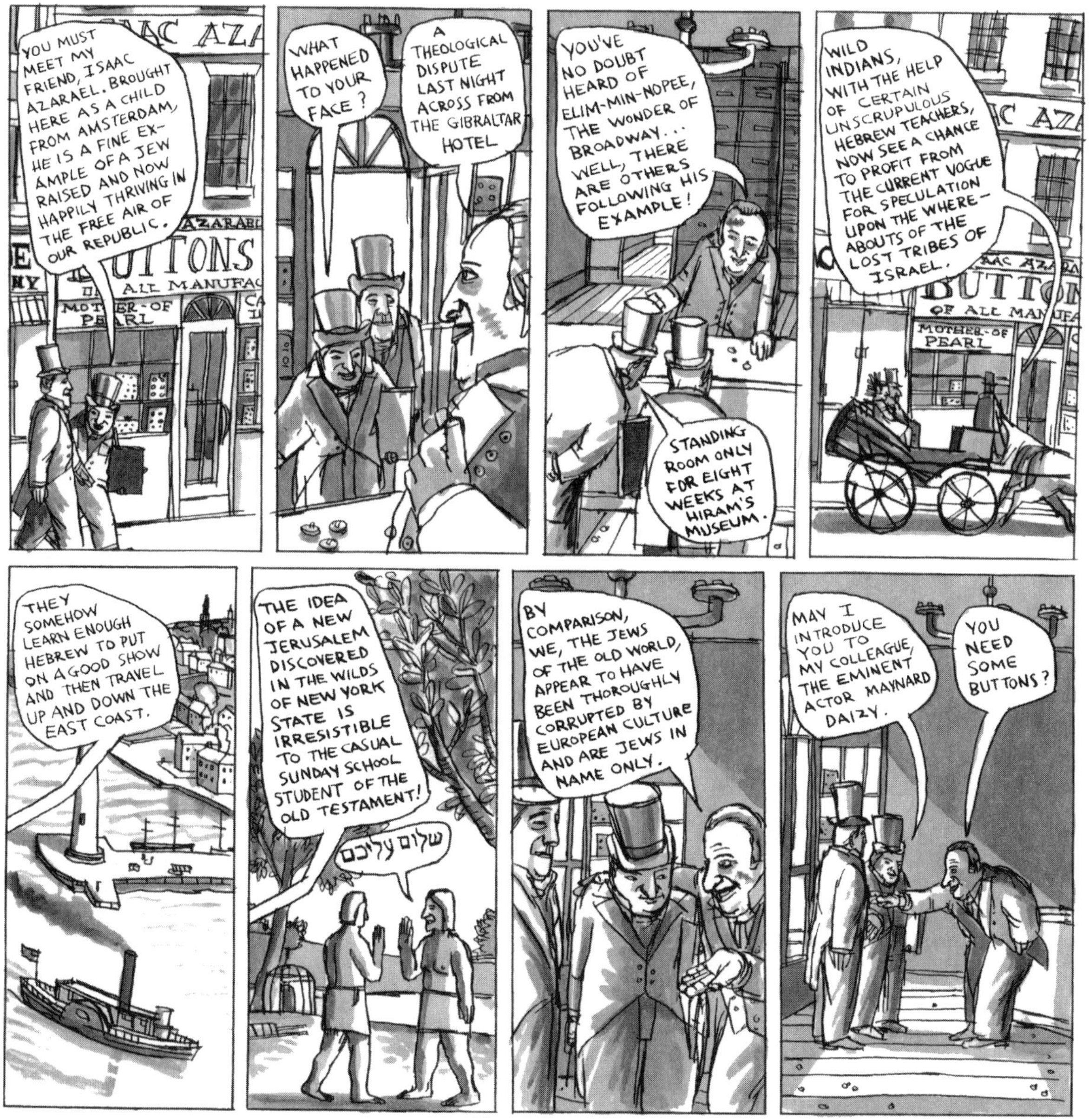
YOU MUST MEET MY FRIEND, ISAAC AZARAEL. BROUGHT HERE AS A CHILD FROM AMSTERDAM, HE IS A FINE EX-AMPLE OF A JEW RAISED AND NOW HAPPILY THRIVING IN THE FREE AIR OF OUR REPUBLIC.
WHAT HAPPENED TO YOUR FACE?
A THEOLOGICAL DISPUTE LAST NIGHT ACROSS FROM THE GIBRALTAR HOTEL
YOU'VE NO DOUBT HEARD OF ELIM-MIN-NOPEE, THE WONDER OF BROADWAY... WELL, THERE ARE OTHERS FOLLOWING HIS EXAMPLE!
STANDING ROOM ONLY FOR EIGHT WEEKS AT HIRAM'S MUSEUM.
WILD INDIANS, WITH THE HELP OF CERTAIN UNSCRUPULOUS HEBREW TEACHERS, NOW SEE A CHANCE TO PROFIT FROM THE CURRENT VOGUE FOR SPECULATION UPON THE WHERE-ABOUTS OF THE LOST TRIBES OF ISRAEL.
THEY SOMEHOW LEARN ENOUGH HEBREW TO PUT ON A GOOD SHOW AND THEN TRAVEL UP AND DOWN THE EAST COAST.
THE IDEA OF A NEW JERUSALEM DISCOVERED IN THE WILDS OF NEW YORK STATE IS IRRESISTIBLE TO THE CASUAL SUNDAY SCHOOL STUDENT OF THE OLD TESTAMENT!
שלום עליכם
BY COMPARISON, WE, THE JEWS OF THE OLD WORLD, APPEAR TO HAVE THOROUGHLY BEEN CORRUPTED BY EUROPEAN CULTURE AND ARE JEWS IN NAME ONLY.
MAY I INTRODUCE YOU TO MY COLLEAGUE, THE EMINENT ACTOR MAYNARD DAIZY.
YOU NEED SOME BUTTONS?

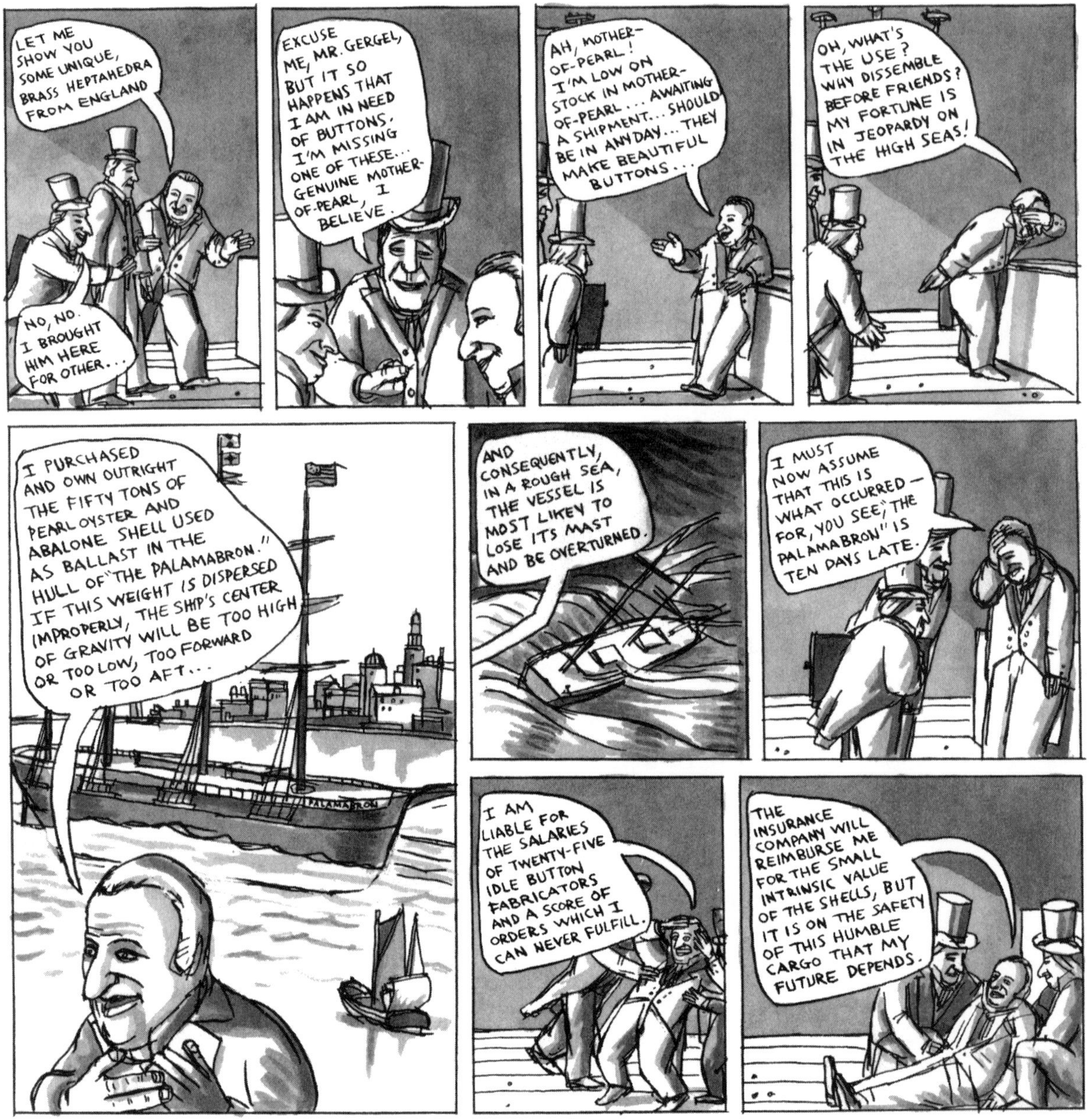
LET ME SHOW YOU SOME UNIQUE, BRASS HEPTAHEDRA FROM ENGLAND
NO, NO. I BROUGHT HIM HERE FOR OTHER...
EXCUSE ME, MR. GERGEL, BUT IT SO HAPPENS THAT I AM IN NEED OF BUTTONS. I'M MISSING ONE OF THESE... GENUINE MOTHER-OF-PEARL, I BELIEVE.
AH, MOTHER-OF-PEARL! I'M LOW ON STOCK IN MOTHER-OF-PEARL... AWAITING A SHIPMENT... SHOULD BE IN ANY DAY... THEY MAKE BEAUTIFUL BUTTONS...
OH, WHAT'S THE USE? WHY DISSEMBLE BEFORE FRIENDS? MY FORTUNE IS IN JEOPARDY ON THE HIGH SEAS!
I PURCHASED AND OWN OUTRIGHT THE FIFTY TONS OF PEARL OYSTER AND ABALONE SHELL USED AS BALLAST IN THE HULL OF "THE PALAMABRON." IF THIS WEIGHT IS DISPERSED IMPROPERLY, THE SHIP'S CENTER OF GRAVITY WILL BE TOO HIGH OR TOO LOW, TOO FORWARD OR TOO AFT...
PALAMABRON
AND CONSEQUENTLY, IN A ROUGH SEA, THE VESSEL IS MOST LIKELY TO LOSE ITS MAST AND BE OVERTURNED.
I MUST NOW ASSUME THAT THIS IS WHAT OCCURRED— FOR, YOU SEE, "THE PALAMABRON" IS TEN DAYS LATE.
I AM LIABLE FOR THE SALARIES OF TWENTY-FIVE IDLE BUTTON FABRICATORS AND A SCORE OF ORDERS WHICH I CAN NEVER FULFILL.
THE INSURANCE COMPANY WILL REIMBURSE ME FOR THE SMALL INTRINSIC VALUE OF THE SHELLS, BUT IT IS ON THE SAFETY OF THIS HUMBLE CARGO THAT MY FUTURE DEPENDS.

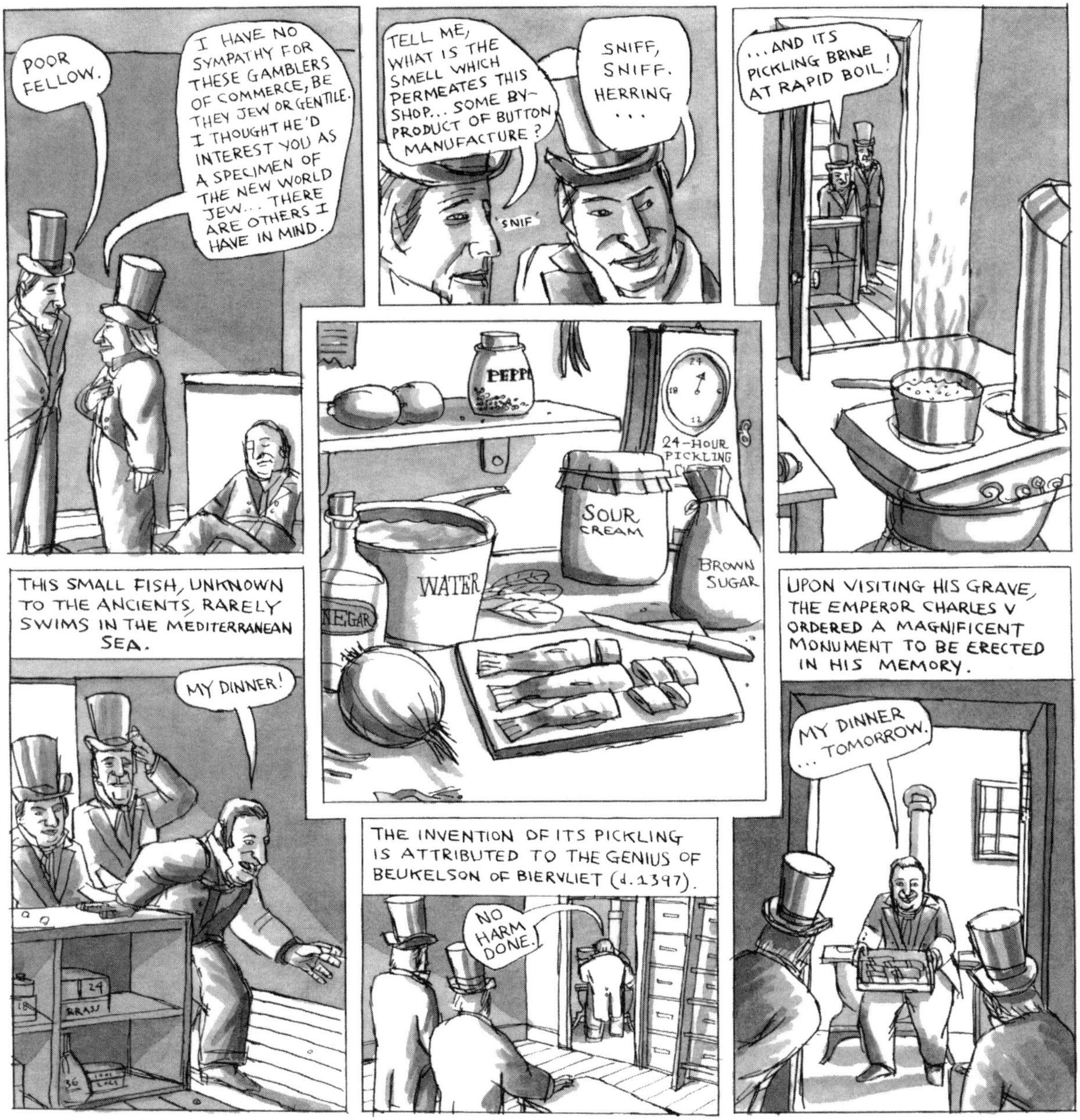
POOR FELLOW.
I HAVE NO SYMPATHY FOR THESE GAMBLERS OF COMMERCE, BE THEY JEW OR GENTILE. I THOUGHT HE'D INTEREST YOU AS A SPECIMEN OF THE NEW WORLD JEW... THERE ARE OTHERS I HAVE IN MIND.
TELL ME, WHAT IS THE SMELL WHICH PERMEATES THIS SHOP... SOME BY-PRODUCT OF BUTTON MANUFACTURE?
SNIF
SNIFF, SNIFF. HERRING . . .
...AND ITS PICKLING BRINE AT RAPID BOIL!
PEPP
24-HOUR PICKLING
SOUR CREAM
WATER
BROWN SUGAR
THIS SMALL FISH, UNKNOWN TO THE ANCIENTS, RARELY SWIMS IN THE MEDITERRANEAN SEA.
MY DINNER!
24
BRASS
UPON VISITING HIS GRAVE, THE EMPEROR CHARLES V ORDERED A MAGNIFICENT MONUMENT TO BE ERECTED IN HIS MEMORY.
MY DINNER ... TOMORROW.
THE INVENTION OF ITS PICKLING IS ATTRIBUTED TO THE GENIUS OF BEUKELSON OF BIERVLIET (d. 1397).
NO HARM DONE.

WITH EACH PASSING DAY, FRANCIS ORIOLE'S DREAM OF CARBONATING LAKE ERIE COMES CLOSER TO REALIZATION.

YOU SEE, A PARTNERSHIP OF LIKE-MINDED BUSINESSMEN CAN ACCOMPLISH WONDERS...

MR. MARAH, OF THE KISHON FUR TRADING CO., HAS PROMISED ONE HUNDRED THOUSAND DOLLARS ... MR. YASCO, OF THE N.Y. SAUSAGE CASING CO., TWENTY-FIVE THOUSAND DOLLARS...

WITH THIS 'SEED MONEY' WE WILL ESTABLISH ONE OFFICE HERE, IN NEW YORK CITY, AND ANOTHER ON THE SHORE OF LAKE ERIE...

AND WITH WHATEVER MONEY'S LEFT OVER, WE'LL TRY TO RENOVATE YOUR WARDROBE. SOMETHING A LITTLE MORE UP-TO-DATE... THE 14th CENTURY, PERHAPS

SAMSON GERGEL INTRODUCES THE EMINENT ACTOR MAYNARD DAIZY TO A NUMBER OF HIS JEWISH FRIENDS.

MR. ELIEZER YASCO, OF THE N.Y. SAUSAGE CASING CO.

MR. GERSHOM LLAMA, TINSMITH.

MR. SHAUL JUVENAL, PRESIDENT OF THE SHEARITH BATSAL BURIAL SOCIETY.

GETTING SOME IDEA OF THE RANGE OF CHARACTER TYPES?

ALMOST ONE THOUSAND JEWS IN THIS CITY ALONE, YOU SAY?

TONIGHT HEBREW RECITATION ELIM-MIN-NOPEE 8 P.M. HIRAM'S MUSEUM

THE THEATER-GOING PUBLIC MAY EXPECT A COMFORTABLY LAUGHABLE CARICATURE OF MAJ. NOAH...

BUT I PROPOSE, THROUGH A SUBTLE FORM OF MIMESIS, TO TURN THE PROSCENIUM ON THEM AND PRESENT THE JEW OF NEW YORK AS I'VE SEEN HIM EXIST IN THE FLESH...

THERE ARE OTHERS I CAN INTRODUCE YOU TO

I WILL FORCE THE AUDIENCE TO SEE ITSELF FROM HIS BELEAGUERED POINT OF VIEW... AS AN ELEGANTLY DRESSED MOB OF JEW-BAITERS.

YOU WILL?

IN THIS REVERSAL OF EXPECTATIONS WILL THE COMEDY LIE.

BRILLIANT!

NEW WORLD THEATER

IT WILL BE A HIGH POINT OF THE THEATER SEASON AND REDOUND TO MY CREDIT AS AN ACTOR.

AS SAMSON GERGEL SUPERVISES THE CONSTRUCTION OF THE PORT OF TUNIS IN PLASTER AND LATHE,

HMM... IMAGINE THE DELICACY OF SUCH AN EFFECT

MAYNARD DAIZY MAKES A CASUAL INQUIRY.

TELL ME, WOULD IT BE POSSIBLE TO INVENT A MECHANISM WHEREBY THE THEATER COULD BE SUFFUSED WITH THE SMELL OF PICKLED HERRING UPON EACH OF MY ENTRANCES?

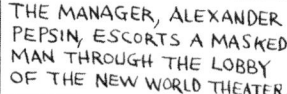

THE MANAGER, ALEXANDER PEPSIN, ESCORTS A MASKED MAN THROUGH THE LOBBY OF THE NEW WORLD THEATER.

LOOK! THE PORT OF TUNIS, ACT II, SCENE 4. DO YOU APPROVE?

YES. VERY GOOD EFFECT.

GENTLEMEN, IT IS MY PLEASURE TO INTRODUCE YOU TO PROF. SOLIDUS, THE AUTHOR OF OUR UPCOMING COMEDY, "THE JEW OF NEW YORK."

THE EMINENT ACTOR, MAYNARD DAIZY, AND OUR SCENIC DESIGNER, SAMSON GERGEL.

LOOKS TO BE A JEW ...AM I RIGHT?

LET ME EXPLAIN... ON THE EUROPEAN CONTINENT, PROF. SOLIDUS' REPUTATION AS A THEORIST AND PAMPHLETEER OF ANTI-SEMITIC SENTIMENTS HAS OVERSHADOWED HIS DELIGHTFUL WORK FOR THE THEATER—COMEDIES, LIBRETTI, ETC.

IN THE EXCITEMENT OF OPENING NIGHT AT THE OBICULAR THEATER IN VIENNA, THE STAGE CURTAINS WERE BURNED AND THREE USHERS WERE MURDERED—YET "DER JUDE FUN NEW YORK" RAN FOR SEVEN HUNDRED CONSECUTIVE NIGHTS.

WE COMMISSIONED AN ENGLISH TRANSLATION AND HOPE TO DUPLICATE THE PLAY'S SUCCESS HERE.

PROF. SOLIDUS, WHO SUFFERS FROM A MORBID FEAR OF PUBLIC HOTELS, WILL BE MAKING HIS HOME, UPSTAIRS, IN MY OFFICE FOR THE DURATION OF HIS STAY IN AMERICA.

I WILL BE HONORED TO ESTABLISH A DEEPER ACQUAINTANCE-SHIP WITH AN ACTOR OF YOUR EMINENCE.

DON'T TAKE IT PERSONALLY, GERGEL.

PROF. SOLIDUS MAKES HIMSELF AT HOME IN THE THIRD FLOOR OFFICE OF THE NEW WORLD THEATER.

KNOCK KNACK KNOCK

THE SOUND OF HAMMERING IN THE STREET INSPIRES HIM TO COMPOSE A NEW ANTI-SEMITIC TRACT.

THE TELLTALE SIGNS OF THE JEW OR CRYPTO-JEW AT WORK ARE VISIBLE, TO THE TRAINED EYE, EVERYWHERE IN THIS YOUNG CITY...

NEW WORLD THEATER

RATHER THAN RISK HIS LIFE IN A PUBLIC DINING ROOM, HE KEEPS A SUPPLY OF DRIED SAUSAGE AND CRACKERS UNDER THE BED.

WHAT TOOK A THOUSAND YEARS TO ACHIEVE IN EUROPE HAS BEEN ACCOMPLISHED HERE IN A FEW DECADES! THE WEB OF ECONOMIC COOPERATION HAS...

KNOCK KNACK

IN THE MIDST OF HIS WORK, HE IS CRIPPLED BY THE PAIN OF INDIGESTION.

ACH!

LAKE ERIE SODA WATER COMPANY

DOWNSTAIRS, SAMSON GERGEL CONFERS WITH THE NEW WORLD THEATER'S MECHANIST, SIGNORE BATTÈLLO.

FOR ME IT'S SIMPLE. ONE PIPE TO THE ORCHESTRA, ONE PIPE TO THE BALCONY!

IN THE CELLAR WE KEEP A CALDRON FULL WITH VINEGAR AND WATER COOKING, COOKING ALL THROUGH THE SHOW. EACH TEN MINUTES WE THROW IN A PIECE OF FISH TO GIVE THAT SMELL.

WHEN I GET THE SIGNAL, I OPEN THE TRAP, THE STEAM SHE GOES UP THE PIPES TO THE ORCHESTRA AND THE BALCONY AND THE PEOPLE HOLD THEIR NOSE.

ON THE NEXT SCENE, I CLOSE THE TRAP. YOU PUT ONE BOY ON THE ROOF AND ONE BOY ON EACH DOOR, THEY OPEN UP AND YOU HAVE THE FRESH AIR... SIMPLE!

[65]

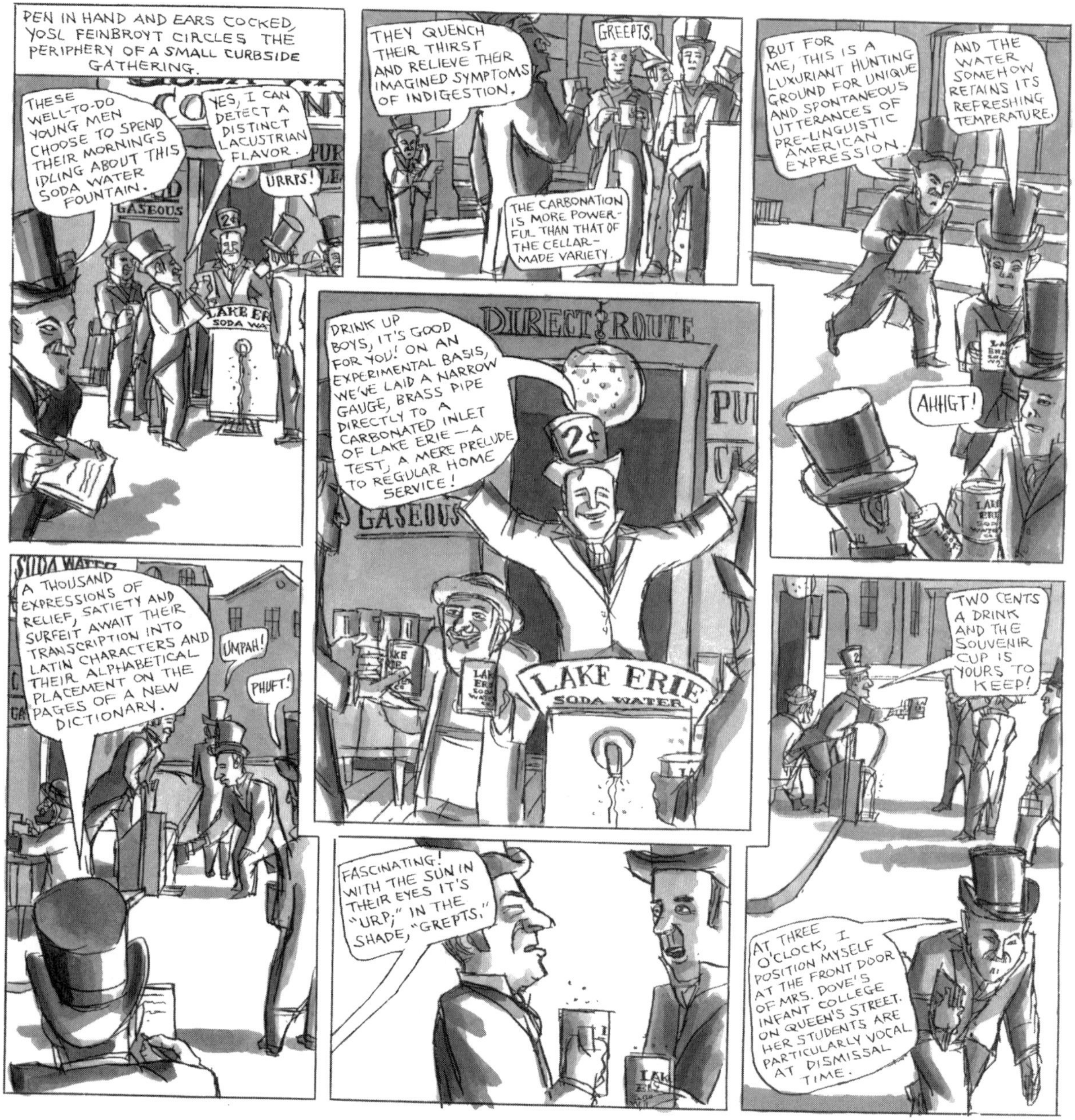
PEN IN HAND AND EARS COCKED, YOSL FEINBROYT CIRCLES THE PERIPHERY OF A SMALL CURBSIDE GATHERING.
THESE WELL-TO-DO YOUNG MEN CHOOSE TO SPEND THEIR MORNINGS IDLING ABOUT THIS SODA WATER FOUNTAIN.
YES, I CAN DETECT A DISTINCT LACUSTRIAN FLAVOR.
URRPS!
GASEOUS
2¢
LAKE ERIE SODA WATER
THEY QUENCH THEIR THIRST AND RELIEVE THEIR IMAGINED SYMPTOMS OF INDIGESTION.
GREEPTS.
THE CARBONATION IS MORE POWERFUL THAN THAT OF THE CELLAR-MADE VARIETY.
BUT FOR ME, THIS IS A LUXURIANT HUNTING GROUND FOR UNIQUE AND SPONTANEOUS UTTERANCES OF PRE-LINGUISTIC AMERICAN EXPRESSION.
AND THE WATER SOMEHOW RETAINS ITS REFRESHING TEMPERATURE.
AHHGT!
DIRECT ROUTE
DRINK UP BOYS, IT'S GOOD FOR YOU! ON AN EXPERIMENTAL BASIS, WE'VE LAID A NARROW GAUGE, BRASS PIPE DIRECTLY TO A CARBONATED INLET OF LAKE ERIE — A TEST, A MERE PRELUDE TO REGULAR HOME SERVICE!
2¢
GASEOUS
LAKE ERIE SODA WATER
A THOUSAND EXPRESSIONS OF RELIEF, SATIETY AND SURFEIT AWAIT THEIR TRANSCRIPTION INTO LATIN CHARACTERS AND THEIR ALPHABETICAL PLACEMENT ON THE PAGES OF A NEW DICTIONARY.
UMPAH!
PHUFT!
TWO CENTS A DRINK AND THE SOUVENIR CUP IS YOURS TO KEEP!
FASCINATING! WITH THE SUN IN THEIR EYES IT'S "URP;" IN THE SHADE, "GREPTS."
AT THREE O'CLOCK, I POSITION MYSELF AT THE FRONT DOOR OF MRS. DOVE'S INFANT COLLEGE ON QUEEN'S STREET. HER STUDENTS ARE PARTICULARLY VOCAL AT DISMISSAL TIME.

NO. CCCX

GALUT'S MINOR DRAMA

THE JEW OF NEW YORK

An Original Comedietta, in Five Acts.

BY PROFESSOR V. SOLIDUS

WITH CAST OF CHARACTERS, STAGE BUSINESS,
COSTUMES, RELATIVE POSITIONS, &c.

NEW YORK
Johnson Galut & Co.
PUBLISHERS
34 QUEEN STREET.

LONDON
Johnson Galut & Co.
PUBLISHERS
219 WHITECHAPEL.

HIRAM'S MUSEUM

No. 472 BROADWAY, BETWEEN GRAND AND BROOME STREETS

EXHIBITIONS OPEN DAY AND NIGHT

A RECITATION

IN PERFECT HEBREW!

BY A RARE AND LIVING MEMBER
OF ONE OF THE LOST TRIBES OF ISRAEL!

ELIM-MIN-NOPEE

RESCUED FROM THE WILDS OF
UPPER NEW YORK STATE!

This prodigy of Nature has been trained to a wonderful degree of intelligence by his Friend and Tutor in the Hebrew Language, Hershel Goulbat.

 Welcoming the Sabbath

PSALMS 45 – 99

AND OTHER INSPIRING HYMNS.

UNDER THE DIRECTION OF MR. GOULBAT, AN AUTHENTIC JEWISH SYNAGOGUE HAS BEEN ERECTED FROM WOOD, AT GREAT EXPENSE, FOR THIS PERFORMANCE.

FRIDAY NIGHT

DOORS OPEN AT 7.

ADMISSION 25 CENTS.

NOW ALSO ON EXHIBITION:
THE WILD SOUTH AMERICAN CREATURE RESPONSIBLE FOR THE DEATH OF THE EMINENT ACTOR MAYNARD DAIZY AND SUBSEQUENTLY DESTROYED.

SOUVENIRS AND REFRESHMENTS ARE AVAILABLE IN THE CHINESE ROOMS ON THE FIRST FLOOR.

IN HIS ROOM ABOVE THE NEW WORLD THEATER, PROF. SOLIDUS MEETS PRIVATELY WITH THE ACTOR MAYNARD DAIZY.

NOW HERE, IN ACT TWO, THE AIR IS THICK WITH THE SMELL OF HERRING AND GABERDINES. MAJOR HAM FEELS THAT HE HAS BEEN BETRAYED BY HIS OWN PEOPLE: THEY DID NOT FOLLOW HIM TO HIS "ARARAT." HIS GRANDIOSE PLAN IS AN UTTER FAILURE.

HE SHEEPISHLY APPROACHES THE FOOTLIGHTS AND ADDRESSES THE AUDIENCE DIRECTLY: "THERE WILL BE NO ACT THREE TO THIS POOR PLAY, MY LOVE OF THEATER HAS GOTTEN IN THE WAY. I TRIED TO SET THE COURSE FOR WANDERING JEWS, LIKE ACTORS WITH A SCRIPT THEY DID NOT CHOOSE. SUCH HUBRIS IN A PLAY GODS TEND TO SMITE, SO I'LL NOT WAIT TO SEE BUT SAY 'GOOD-NIGHT.'"

THE CURTAIN FALLS! WHAT DO YOU THINK? IN BERLIN WE HAD RIOTS! THEY PAID FOR A FULL EVENING'S ENTERTAINMENT, OR AT LEAST THREE ACTS WORTH, AND VIOLENTLY DEMANDED THEIR MONEY BACK — CHRISTIAN AND JEW ALIKE!

YOU SEE THOSE FELLOWS ACROSS THE STREET? ONE OF THEM'S AN ORIENTAL JEW—THEY'VE DEVISED A SCHEME WHEREBY THEY CAN CHARGE PEOPLE TWO CENTS FOR A DRINK OF WATER, CAN YOU IMAGINE, MAKING A BUSINESS OUT OF WHAT FALLS FREELY FROM THE SKY? WHAT'S NEXT, THE AIR WE BREATHE?

YOU SEE, I HAVE BECOME AN EXPERT TAXONOMIST OF THE JEW IN ALL HIS MYRIAD FORMS. I KNOW MORE OF THEIR RELIGIOUS OBLIGATIONS THAN THEY DO THEM- SELVES. I KNOW WHAT THEY LIKE TO EAT, THEIR FAVORITE TERMS OF ENDEARMENT AND ALL OF THEIR LANGUAGES.

BUT HERE, IN AMERICA, THROUGH ASSIMILATION AND INTERMARRIAGE, I FEAR THAT SOMEDAY ALL OF THESE TRAITS WILL BECOME DIFFUSED WITHIN THE GENERAL POPULATION—AND IN THAT, THE REAL DANGER LIES! THERE WILL BE NO JEWS LEFT, AS I KNOW THEM, TO WRITE ABOUT.

OF COURSE, I CAN RETURN TO THE WORLD OF OPERETTA WITH ITS ENGLISHMEN, FRENCHMEN AND AFRICAN NATIVES — BUT IT'S NOT THE SAME. WITHOUT THE JUDEO-CHRISTIAN ETHOS AS A BACKDROP, ALL YOU HAVE IS CHEAP BURLESQUE.

A LETTER FOR MR. MARAH

AH, AT LAST! A PURCHASE ORDER! 2,500 PELTS TO BE SHIPPED TO LIVERPOOL ON THE FIRST OF THE MONTH.

I'VE IMPORTED PHYLACTERIES FROM THE FARTHEST CORNERS OF THE EARTH WITH LITTLE TROUBLE... BUT PELTS FROM AN UNSPECIFIED ICE HOUSE IN BUFFALO, N.Y.? I NEED PARTICULARS. I MUST HAVE THE MERCHANDISE IN HAND.

AND LOOK AT MY PARTNER — A POTENTIALLY WEALTHY YOUNG MAN — LYING IN THE STREET WITHOUT HIS TROUSERS.

BY SHEER LUCK HE'S AMASSED A FORTUNE IN BEAVER PELTS, BUT HAS, IN THE PROCESS, LOST HIS DESIRE TO ENJOY THE FRUITS OF SOCIETY.

WITH MY SMALL COMMISSION FROM THIS SALE, I WILL RENT A SUITE OF ROOMS IN THE AMERICAN HOTEL AND THERE MINGLE, ON A NIGHTLY BASIS, WITH THE CREAM OF SOCIETY. MY WEALTH WILL BEGET MORE WEALTH.

I'VE WASTED THE LAST FIVE YEARS OF MY LIFE DEALING IN RELIGIOUS ARTICLES. PEOPLE TODAY FIND SPIRITUAL SOLACE IN BALLROOM DANCING.

COME, NUSIN... WHERE ARE YOUR TROUSERS? AREN'T YOU COLD? WHO KNOWS WHAT DISEASE BREEDS IN THIS DAMP RIVER AIR? THE LOSS BY CHOLERA TO SLAVE OWNERS IN LOUISIANA WAS ESTIMATED AT FOUR MILLION DOLLARS. COME, WE HAVE BUSINESS TO ATTEND TO.

TO ENTRUST OUR FIRST SHIPMENT OF PELTS TO A COMMERCIAL FREIGHT HANDLER WOULD BE IMPRUDENT. THE BANKS OF THE ERIE CANAL ARE LINED WITH THIEVES WHO KNOW WHAT'S ON EVERY BOAT. SOMEONE MUST ESCORT THE PELTS FROM BUFFALO TO NEW YORK CITY AND LOOK OUT FOR OUR INTERESTS.

AS YOU'RE IN NO CONDITION TO UNDERTAKE SUCH A JOURNEY, I MUST BE THE ONE. I'LL ESTABLISH A DEPENDABLE SYSTEM FOR THE FUTURE. I'LL MAKE FRIENDS AMONG THE BARGEMEN. I'LL LET THE THIEVES KNOW THAT THEY'RE DEALING WITH THE KISHON FUR TRADING COMPANY!

SIGN THESE LETTERS OF CONVEYANCE—ONE TO THE AURORA ICE HOUSE OF BUFFALO, NEW YORK, AND ONE TO THE TCHUKTCHIS BARGE COMPANY OF ALBANY. I'LL LEAVE TONIGHT.

YOU'RE RIGHT, I'M IN NO CONDITION TO MAKE SUCH A DANGEROUS TRIP.

STAY HERE UNTIL I RETURN. I'M EXPECTING A SHIPMENT OF TEFILLIN FROM PALESTINE NEXT WEEK. I TRUST YOU. AFTER ALL... WE'RE PARTNERS.

SO, FOR A PALTRY FIFTEEN PERCENT I'M TO RISK MY LIFE ESTABLISHING THE KISHON FUR TRADING COMPANY. I KNOW THIS A BUSINESS ARRANGEMENT, BUT IT'S SIMPLY NOT FAIR!

ON AN IMPULSE, MR. MARAH ENTERS THE AMERICAN HOTEL ON BROADWAY...

I WANT THE BEST ROOM YOU HAVE... FOR TWO WEEKS!

HE SUMMONS A MESSENGER...

HERE, TAKE THIS LETTER TO THE NEW YORK OFFICE OF THE TCHUKTCHIS BARGE COMPANY, 24 CROWN STREET, BY THE RIVER.

YOUR ROOM IS READY.

IF IT MAKES KISHON HAPPY, LET HIM THINK THAT I'M RISKING MY LIFE FOR HIS BENEFIT.

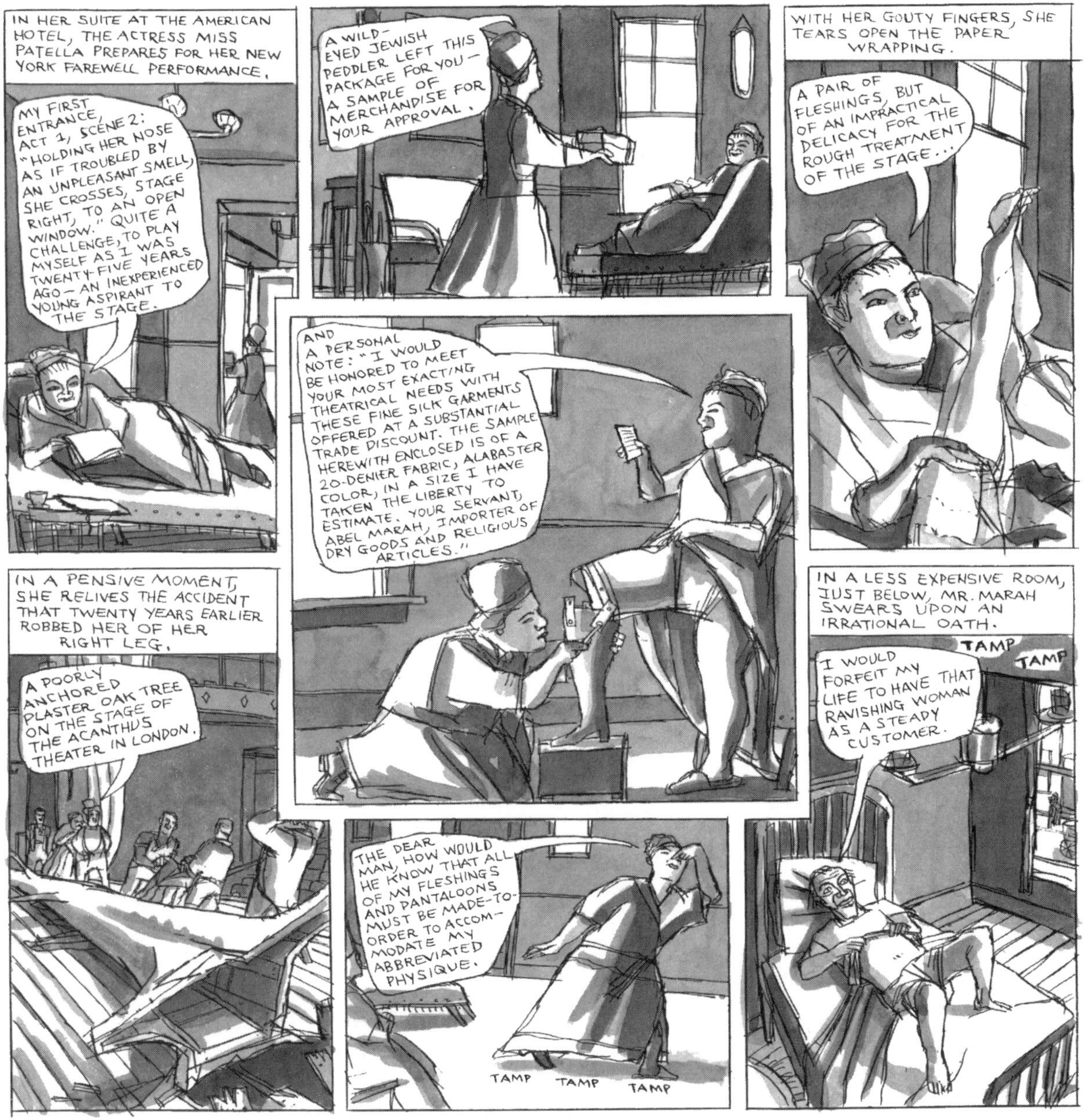

IN HER SUITE AT THE AMERICAN HOTEL, THE ACTRESS MISS PATELLA PREPARES FOR HER NEW YORK FAREWELL PERFORMANCE.
MY FIRST ENTRANCE, ACT 1, SCENE 2: "HOLDING HER NOSE AS IF TROUBLED BY AN UNPLEASANT SMELL, SHE CROSSES, STAGE RIGHT, TO AN OPEN WINDOW." QUITE A CHALLENGE, TO PLAY MYSELF AS I WAS TWENTY-FIVE YEARS AGO — AN INEXPERIENCED YOUNG ASPIRANT TO THE STAGE.
A WILD-EYED JEWISH PEDDLER LEFT THIS PACKAGE FOR YOU — A SAMPLE OF MERCHANDISE FOR YOUR APPROVAL.
WITH HER GOUTY FINGERS, SHE TEARS OPEN THE PAPER WRAPPING.
A PAIR OF FLESHINGS, BUT OF AN IMPRACTICAL DELICACY FOR THE ROUGH TREATMENT OF THE STAGE...
AND A PERSONAL NOTE: "I WOULD BE HONORED TO MEET YOUR MOST EXACTING THEATRICAL NEEDS WITH THESE FINE SILK GARMENTS OFFERED AT A SUBSTANTIAL TRADE DISCOUNT. THE SAMPLE HEREWITH ENCLOSED IS OF A 20-DENIER FABRIC, ALABASTER COLOR, IN A SIZE I HAVE TAKEN THE LIBERTY TO ESTIMATE. YOUR SERVANT, ABEL MARAH, IMPORTER OF DRY GOODS AND RELIGIOUS ARTICLES."
IN A PENSIVE MOMENT, SHE RELIVES THE ACCIDENT THAT TWENTY YEARS EARLIER ROBBED HER OF HER RIGHT LEG.
A POORLY ANCHORED PLASTER OAK TREE ON THE STAGE OF THE ACANTHUS THEATER IN LONDON.
THE DEAR MAN, HOW WOULD HE KNOW THAT ALL OF MY FLESHINGS AND PANTALOONS MUST BE MADE-TO-ORDER TO ACCOMMODATE MY ABBREVIATED PHYSIQUE.
TAMP TAMP TAMP
IN A LESS EXPENSIVE ROOM, JUST BELOW, MR. MARAH SWEARS UPON AN IRRATIONAL OATH.
TAMP TAMP
I WOULD FORFEIT MY LIFE TO HAVE THAT RAVISHING WOMAN AS A STEADY CUSTOMER.

A LETTER FOR MR. MARAH.

A PROMPT CONFIRMATION OF MY ORDER... "THE TCHUKTCHIS BARGE CO. WILL UNDERTAKE TO TRANSFER 2,500 BEAVER PELTS FROM THE AURORA ICE HOUSE IN BUFFALO, N.Y., TO THE CROWN STREET WHARF, MANHATTAN ON OR BEFORE AUGUST 31ST."

THERE, IT'S AS GOOD AS DONE! OF COURSE THERE ARE RISKS INVOLVED IN TRANSPORTING SUCH A VALUABLE CARGO ACROSS THE WILDS OF NEW YORK STATE, BUT WHY SHOULD I ADD MY LIFE TO THE SUM OF OUR LIABILITIES?

I'M BETTER OFF HERE, AT THE HEART OF THINGS. I HAVE OTHER SALES PENDING. I WILL CONDUCT MY BUSINESS, FOR THE NEXT TWO WEEKS, FROM THIS HOTEL BED. LET NATHAN KISHON IMAGINE THE HARDSHIPS I'M ENDURING.

EACH NIGHT, MR. MARAH'S SLEEP IS DISRUPTED BY THE SOUND OF HEBREW READINGS...

THE SAME THING OVER AND OVER AGAIN... A HUNDRED TIMES...

כִּי־תוֹלִיד בָּנִים וּבְנֵי בָנִים וְנוֹשַׁנְתֶּם בָּאָרֶץ...

QUIET! ENOUGH! IT'S ONE O'CLOCK IN THE MORNING! SAY AMEN ALREADY!

כִּי־תוֹלִיד בָּנִים וּבְנֵי בָנִים...

IN THE ROOM BELOW, HERSHEL GOULBAT COACHES ÉLIM-MIN-NOPEE IN A NEW SET OF RECITATIONS...

GO ON, ONE MORE TIME. IT'S STILL EARLY! REMEMBER, OUR SPECIAL TISHOH B'OV SHOW OPENS NEXT WEEK. THE AUDIENCE EXPECTS NEW MATERIAL.

כִּי־תוֹלִיד בָּנִים וּבְנֵי בָנִים...

I WOULD LIKE TO GO DOWN THERE RIGHT NOW BUT I CAN'T RISK A PUBLIC ALTERCATION INVOLVING A CO-RELIGIONIST. IT'S A SMALL COMMUNITY ... KISHON MIGHT GET WIND OF IT AND I'M SUPPOSED TO BE OUT OF TOWN.

כִּי־תוֹלִיד בָּנִים...

MR. MARAH RELAXES IN HIS ROOM IN THE AMERICAN HOTEL ON BROADWAY.

JUST NOW I'D BE ARRIVING IN BUFFALO, EXHAUSTED, AT THE MERCY OF THIEVES AND SWINDLERS. THEY'D SEE FOR THEM-SELVES THAT I WAS AN EASY MARK... WAIT UNTIL NIGHTFALL, AND THEN, WITH NO COMPUNCTION, FINISH ME OFF AND BE RICHER BY 2,500 PELTS.

IT WOULD BE A TRAGEDY, BUT THESE THINGS HAPPEN... HMM? ... WHERE'S THAT MESSENGER?

A HALF AN HOUR LATER...

LETTER FOR MR. NATHAN KISHON

THE MANAGEMENT OF THE NIAGRA HOTEL OF BUFFALO, N.Y., MUST REGRET-FULLY INFORM YOU THAT YOUR PARTNER AND DEAR FRIEND, MR. ABEL MARAH, WAS FOUND DEAD ON THE EVENING OF AUG. 15th IN HIS BED (ROOM 12), THE APPARENT VICTIM OF A ROBBERY. IT MAY LIGHTEN THE BURDEN OF YOUR GRIEF TO KNOW THAT THE DISPOSITION OF MR.MARAH'S BODY, AT THE TIME OF ITS DISCOVERY, INDICATED THAT HE LOST HIS LIFE IN THE HEROIC DEFENSE OF A QUANTITY OF BEAVER PELTS. THE WHEREABOUTS OF THE MURDERERS AND THE PELTS ARE UNKNOWN AT PRESENT. WITH OUR CONDOLENCES, THE MANAGEMENT.

NATHAN KISHON WANDERS TOWARD SHEARITH BATSAL IN SEARCH OF A FAMILIAR FACE.

A STRANGER OFFERS HIM A BISCUIT.

I COME HERE EVERY DAY AFTER THE SERVICE FOR A LITTLE SOMETHING TO EAT

SHAUL JUVENAL FROM THE BURIAL SOCIETY, HAVE YOU SEEN HIM?

OH, I'M SORRY... WAS IT YOUR WIFE OR AN AGED FATHER? PERHAPS WE CAN INFLUENCE THE COURSE OF THEIR TRANSMIGRATION... HELP SHORTEN THEIR WANDERINGS...

IT WAS MY BUSINESS PARTNER.

MY NAME IS YOSL FEINBROYT, LET ME EXAMINE YOUR FOREHEAD.

[73]

YOU SEE, THERE EXISTS, UNBEKNOWNST TO US, A COMMUNITY OF SOULS WORKING ON OUR BEHALF. IT'S SIMPLY A MATTER OF IDENTIFYING WHERE YOU FIT IN.

NOTHING... AN UNFURROWED FOREHEAD... NO INDICATION OF YOUR SOUL'S JOURNEY... AH, WAIT... HERE... I SEE SOMETHING... A BULLOCK RUBBING ITS FLANK AGAINST THE BARK OF A TREE!

I CAN SEE INTO THE FOUR CHAMBERS OF ITS STOMACH. A QUANTITY OF GRASS SWALLOWED, UNCHEWED, INTO THE LARGEST CHAMBER WHERE IT LIES, FERMENTING AND THEN, AFTER A TIME, I SEE IT REGURGITATED TO BE CHEWED FOR THE FIRST TIME AND THEN SWALLOWED AGAIN...

BUT INSTEAD OF PASSING ON TO THE DIGESTIVE CHAMBER IT RETURNS AGAIN TO LIE IN THE FIRST CHAMBER, ONLY TO BE REGURGITATED AGAIN AT A LATER TIME...

FEINBROYT, HE ALWAYS SHOWS UP IN TIME FOR THE CAKE, BISCUITS AND WINE.

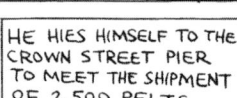

The contents of Mr. Marah's desk drawer
1. Assorted leather straps
2. A Haggadah in the Iroquois language
3. A Masonic pin
4. A half-dozen miniature scrolls of blank parchment
5. A series of French boudoir prints hidden in a phylactery bag
6. A wax esrog
7. A map of Odessa

TEN DAYS LATER MR. MARAH CHECKS OUT OF THE AMERICAN HOTEL

AT SEVEN O'CLOCK, THE SHIP SETS SAIL AND MR. MARAH REGRETS NOT HAVING HAD ONE LAST CHANCE TO GO THROUGH HIS DESK DRAWER.

AMERICAN HOTEL

HE HIES HIMSELF TO THE CROWN STREET PIER TO MEET THE SHIPMENT OF 2,500 PELTS.

HE'S SHOWN TO HIS CABIN AND MAKES SMALL TALK WITH A DECK HAND.

JUST THINK, THE LOSS BY CHOLERA TO SLAVE OWNERS IN LOUISIANA WAS ESTIMATED AT FOUR MILLION DOLLARS.

ENOCH LETUSHIM, NOW DRESSED IN THE LATEST STYLE OF CUTAWAY JACKET AND FULL-LENGTH TROUSERS, ACCOMPANIES FRANCIS ORIOLE ON A SERIES OF AFTERNOON BUSINESS CALLS.

I SAY KEEP THE TURBAN... IT GIVES YOU AN AIR OF ORIENTAL REFINEMENT.

OUR FIRST STOP IS THE OFFICE OF MR. MARAH. I EXPECT HE'LL HAVE A BANK DRAFT WAITING FOR US TODAY.

WHAT'S THIS? AH, HOW I HATE TO SEE FUNERAL CREPE ON SUCH A GLORIOUS SUMMER DAY... MR. MARAH'S OFFICE IS ON THE SECOND FLOOR.

A SMALL, HANDWRITTEN NOTICE, PINNED TO THE DOOR, SADLY INFORMS THE PUBLIC OF MR. MARAH'S UNTIMELY DEATH.

WHAT WAS HE DOING IN BUFFALO?? PERHAPS HE LEFT WORD WITH HIS BANK?

ENOCH LETUSHIM'S THOUGHTS TURN, FOR A MOMENT, TO THE TRADE HE HAD RECENTLY ALL BUT RENOUNCED.

WE'VE BEEN ROBBED OF A KEY INVESTOR. THIS IS A SETBACK... THE OTHERS ARE NOW LIKELY TO GET COLD FEET.

I WONDER, WILL THEY SEND THE BODY BACK? WHERE'S THE FAMILY?

PERHAPS WE SHOULD SPEND A FEW HOURS TONIGHT IN THE LOBBY OF THE AMERICAN HOTEL? THERE'S A BIG PARTY TONIGHT, YOU NEVER KNOW WHAT OPPORTUNITY MAY ARISE.

DID HE LEAVE ANY SPECIFIC BURIAL REQUESTS?

THEN IT'S AGREED... WE MEET TONIGHT IN THE LOBBY OF THE AMERICAN HOTEL!

I HAVE A FEW FRESH BAGS LEFT UNDER MY BED...

ENOCH LETUSHIM RETURNS TO HIS HOTEL ROOM AND MAKES A COMPLETE INVENTORY OF HIS STOCK OF SOIL FROM THE HOLY LAND.

...SEVEN FULL... THREE HALF-FULL AND ANOTHER QUARTER OF A BAG TO BE SWEPT UP FROM THE FLOOR.

AT A DRESS REHEARSAL OF THE SEASON'S NEW COMEDY, "THE JEW OF NEW YORK,"

MAY I HAVE THE PLEASURE OF INTRODUCING YOU TO ONE OF OUR FINEST YOUNG ACTRESSES...

SAMSON GERGEL SITS IN THE BALCONY TO BETTER TAKE IN THE ENTIRE TABLEAU.

MISS PATELLA, MAJOR HAM

MY PLEASURE, INDEED.

WITH EACH NEW SCENE, THE DEFECTS BECOME MORE APPARENT.

FLAT! EVERYTHING APPEARS FLAT AS PAPER... LIKE A CHILD'S CUTOUT.

YOO-HOO MISS PATELLA!

IF THE SPECTATOR SHIFTS, EVEN EVER SO SLIGHTLY, IN HIS SEAT, HE CAN SEE THROUGH TO EVERYTHING TO THE EMPTY WALL AT THE BACK OF THE STAGE.

AND THE LIGHT... IT'S ALL WRONG! THE SUNSET OVER THE BAY OF TUNIS IS LIKE A DIRTY OIL LAMP!

THE EPISCOPAL CHURCH OF BUFFALO, EIGHT HUNDRED DOLLARS WORTH OF LATHE AND PLASTER ...ALL FOR NOTHING!

AT EACH OF MAYNARD DAIZY'S ENTRANCES, THE THEATER IS FILLED WITH THE SMELL OF PICKLED HERRING.

PEW! AN UNNECESSARY AND VULGAR EFFECT.

AS THE FINAL CURTAIN FALLS, THE AUTHOR, PROF. SOLIDUS, LEAPS TO HIS FEET.

BRAVO! BRAVO! A MASTERFUL PRODUCTION! I COULD ALMOST SMELL THE FILTHY LITTLE CHARACTERS!

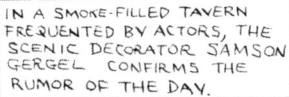

IN A SMOKE-FILLED TAVERN FREQUENTED BY ACTORS, THE SCENIC DECORATOR SAMSON GERGEL CONFIRMS THE RUMOR OF THE DAY.

AS A PROFESSIONAL COURTESY, SOLIDUS INVITED MAJOR NOAH TO ATTEND THIS AFTERNOON'S DRESS REHEARSAL.

THE BRAZENNESS OF THE MAN!

YES, POOR MAJOR NOAH SAT PATIENTLY THROUGH THE ENTIRE PLAY, LAUGHED POLITELY AT THE INTENDED MOMENTS, AND AFTERWARDS CONGRATULATED THE AUTHOR ON HIS ACCOMPLISHMENT.

BY PLACING YOUR DENOUEMENT IN THE SECOND ACT YOU'VE RENDERED THE LAST THREE ACTS SUPERFLUOUS.

"BREVITY IS THE SOUL OF WIT."

HE QUOTED A SINGLE LINE WHICH HE RECOGNIZED AS AN ALLUSION TO A WORK BY MARLOWE.

"BUT STAY, WHAT NOSE SHINES YONDER IN THE EAST?"

MOST IGNORAMUSES THINK OF SHAKESPEARE.

HE REFUSED TO LET ON THAT HE WAS THE BUTT OF THE COMEDY AND INSTEAD OFFERED AN IMPROMPTU ANALYSIS OF THE STAGE JEW.

YOUR JEW OF NEW YORK COULD ONLY EXIST ON THE STAGE ALONGSIDE OTHER STOCK COMIC FIGURES — A MALEVOLENT PUNCHINELLO WHO WALKS ABROAD A-NIGHT TO KILL SICK PEOPLE AND POISON WELLS.

AN AMERICAN AUDIENCE WOULD NOT RECOGNIZE HIM AS A CREATURE OF FLESH AND BLOOD CAPABLE OF WENDING HIS WAY THROUGH THE POLITICAL INTRIGUES YOU'VE INVENTED.

AS FOR MY DEAR FRIEND, THE ACTOR MAYNARD DAIZY, HIS STOOP WAS NOT PRONOUNCED ENOUGH. I DID NOT KNOW IF I SHOULD LAUGH OR HAVE PITY ON HIM.

YOU SEE, JUST WHAT I SAID.

AND, OF COURSE, I WILL RETURN ON OPENING NIGHT TO WITNESS MISS PATELLA'S FAREWELL PERFORMANCE — THE PLAY THAT EVENING IS IMMATERIAL.

SOLIDUS THANKED MAJOR NOAH FOR HIS CRITIQUE AND THEN CONFESSED, AS A FELLOW PLAYWRIGHT, THAT HE HAD SOME TREPIDATION CONCERNING THE REACTION OF AN AMERICAN AUDIENCE TO HIS WORK. IN BERLIN, HE SAID, THEY HAD RIOTS.

LIKELY STORY.

THAT SAME AFTERNOON, YOSL FEINBROYT VISITS THE PUBLISHER OF A NEW AMERICAN DICTIONARY.

MR. CHAMPEEN WILL SEE YOU NOW.

I HAVE HERE A CATALOG OF SIX HUNDRED ECHOIC WORDS DERIVED FROM THE PROCESSES OF EATING AND DIGESTION — A COMPLETELY IGNORED REALM OF HUMAN DISCOURSE. THESE ORPHANED WORDS MUST BE GIVEN THEIR RIGHTFUL PLACE IN THE AMERICAN LANGUAGE.

SEVENTY-FIVE VERBS, SUCH AS "ZHALOUP," "CHOUP" AND "SZLIPS," TO DESCRIBE THE ENTRY OF VARIOUS FOODSTUFFS INTO THE HUMAN MOUTH, COMPLETE WITH DEFINITIONS, A KEY TO USAGE AND PRECISE ETYMOLOGIES.

VERY NOVEL, BUT WHO AMONG US RECOGNIZES THESE WORDS?

EIGHTY-TWO WORDS, SUCH AS "KEYAP," "CHIKUS" AND "GARAPIS," TO DELINEATE THE MASTICATION OF SOLID FOOD.

OUR DICTIONARIES ARE INTENDED FOR THE GENERAL ANGLO-AMERICAN SPEAKING PUBLIC.

ONE HUNDRED AND SEVEN WORDS, SUCH AS "UKIFT," "UMPUCT" AND "FERVELS," WITH WHICH TO CHARACTERIZE THE SWILLING AND SWALLOWING OF DRINK AND SOUPS.

THANK YOU FOR TAKING THE TIME TO VISIT...

ONE HUNDRED AND THIRTY WORDS, SUCH AS "GREPTS," "YOUCHS" AND "HARZS," TO DESCRIBE ONE'S RELIEF FOLLOWING A BOUT OF INDIGESTION.

BUT YOUR WORK TRANSCENDS THE SCOPE OF OUR MODEST PROJECT.

THE PUBLISHER STOPS TO LISTEN AS FEINBROYT, STANDING IN THE NOISY STREET, READS HIS ENTRY FOR THE WORD "GREPTS."

"THERE IS WRITTEN PROOF THAT SINCE THE 17th CENTURY THE WORD "RÜLPSEN" WAS USED FOR LOUD BURPING (ONOMATOPOEIC). FROM RÜZ (MID-HIGH GERMAN), A PEASANT, A BOOR, IN A NEGATIVE SENSE, A LOUT. SOUND IMITATING ORIGIN. SEE AUFSTOSZEN. AMONGST JUDEO-GERMAN SPEAKERS WITHIN EASTERN EUROPE, THE WORD "GREPTS," A LOCAL REFINEMENT OF THE EARLIER WORD, CAME TO DESCRIBE THE ORAL ERUCTATION CAUSED BY THEIR PARTICULAR CUISINE. ITS FIRST AMERICAN USAGE WAS NOTED IN 1830 AT THE CHALDEAN BEER GARDEN IN THE CITY OF NEW YORK."

ANOTHER RUMOR STARTS AS A SENTENCE WRITTEN BY AN ANONYMOUS WIT ON THE SECOND PAGE OF A DAILY NEWSPAPER.

"ELIM-MIN-NOPEE, THE HEBREW-SPEAKING INDIAN AND CURRENT ATTRACTION AT HIRAM'S MUSEUM ON BROADWAY, IS PLANNING TO GO ON TOUR THIS FALL DIS-GUISED AS A JEW SPECIALIZING IN KNIFE THROWING.!"

WITHIN DAYS, PEOPLE BEGIN TO TALK...

PAY TO SEE A JEW MASQUERADING AS AN INDIAN? WHY YOU CAN HEAR THE SAME RECITATIONS, FREE OF CHARGE, AT THE PALP STREET SYNAGOGUE.

AND IF HE IS A GENUINE INDIAN, AND A MEMBER OF SOME LOST HEBREW TRIBE, HE CERTAINLY ISN'T LOST ANY LONGER!

HE HAS A SUITE AT THE AMERICAN HOTEL.

ON THAT FRIDAY NIGHT, THE AUDITORIUM IS HALF EMPTY.

INSTEAD OF WATCHING THE TICKET SALES DWINDLE OVER THE NEXT THREE WEEKS, MR. HIRAM OFFERS GOULBAT AND HIS "INDIAN" A SUM OF MONEY TO END THEIR ENGAGEMENT PREMATURELY.

THE STAGE SYNAGOGUE IS PACKED INTO THREE CRATES AND SHIPPED TO PHILADELPHIA.

NEW POSTERS ARE PRINTED WHICH STRESS ELIM-MIN-NOPEE'S "WILD" AND "UNCIVILIZED" NATURE.

ELIM-MIN-NOPEE
A RARE LIVING SPECIMEN
RESCUED FROM NATURE
WILD
PERFECT HEBREW
UNCIVILIZED UNTIL NOW!!

THE SHOW AT THE SCIENTIFIC MUSEUM IN PHILADELPHIA OPENS WITH THE CRACK OF A WHIP AND THE ROAR OF A CAGED MAN.

CRAC!

GRRROOO

CHAS. LORGNETTE

Cordially Invites the Businessmen, Actors, Private Fanciers and
Other Interested Parties to Examine his

FASCINATING STOCK

OF

 PARISIAN

Assorted, 20 Denier

FLESHINGS,

Manufactured for Professional Theatrical Function

Recently Imported From France, these Garments Represent the Latest Improvements in Design and Translucency of Silken Fabric. From the Stage, they have been Attested to Produce the Unquestionable Illusion of the Unclad Human Form in All Its Glory.

THE INVENTORY OF

Arabian Harem Slippers.
Extra-Tight Cambric Shirts.
British Fox-Hunting Pants.
Chinese Opium Caps.
Fancy Half-Pants.
Disposable Venus Cups.

Gentlemen's and Ladies'
Perspiration Pillows.
Grecian Houseboy Uniforms.
Roman Catholic Clerical Vestments
in Young Women's sizes.
And Other Specialty Dry Goods.

CHARLES LORGNETTE,
Proprietor and licensed importer

VINOPER AND SUNCH, PRINTERS AND WASTE-PAPER
HANDLERS, BOWERY

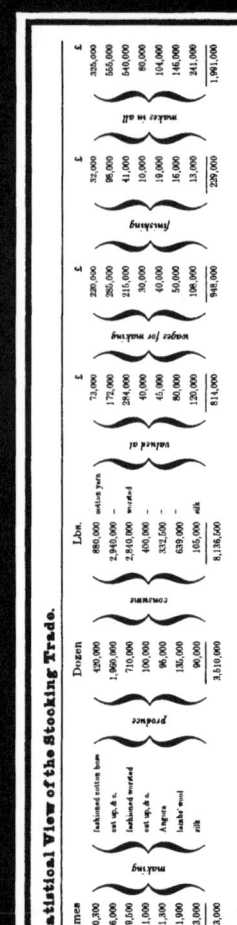

Statistical View of the Stocking Trade.

HOW WAS IT POSSIBLE, IN THE GARDEN OF EDEN, FOR THE DEVIL TO SEDUCE EVE, A WOMAN, WHILE IN THE FORM OF A SERPENT?

THEOLOGIANS SPECULATE THAT THE SERPENT MOVED IN AN ERECT POSTURE PRIOR TO THE FALL AND MAY HAVE BEEN ENDOWED WITH OTHER HUMAN ATTRIBUTES.

A PAIL OF APPLESAUCE, PLEASE.

MAURICE KETZELBOURD, NOW ON HIS OWN, CEASED TO TROUBLE HIMSELF WITH THE FURTHERANCE OF HIS BUSINESS AFFAIRS.

CAN YOU IMAGINE, I ONCE LEASED ALL OF MY EQUIPMENT FROM THAT MAN.

WITH A DEGREE OF ABANDON RARELY ACHIEVED BY MAN, HE GIVES HIMSELF OVER TO THE HUMBLE PASSIONS OF AN ANIMAL.

MISS PATELLA AS FRIAR MACAQUE IN "THE MARZIPAN SAINT."

BUT AN ANIMAL CAPABLE OF READING A NEWSPAPER

"ON SEPTEMBER 10th, MISS PATELLA WILL MAKE HER NEW YORK FAREWELL APPEARANCE IN PROF. SOLIDUS'S "THE JEW OF NEW YORK." THE VETERAN ACTRESS FACES THE FORMIDABLE TASK OF PLAYING HERSELF AS A YOUNG WOMAN."

SHOO!

AND HANDLING MONEY.

TWO HUNDRED DOLLARS IN TEN DOLLAR BILLS, PLEASE.

AN ANIMAL WITH THE POWERS OF LOGIC AND WHEREWITHAL TO BUY A COACH TICKET TO NEW YORK CITY

AND ASK DIRECTIONS OF A STRANGER.

THE HOTEL GIBRALTAR?

ACTING UPON A DIM MEMORY OF HUMAN COMPORTMENT, MOISHE KETZELBOURD MANAGES TO REGISTER AT THE DESK OF A HOTEL.

AH, COUGAR— OF FRENCH DESCENT?

YES, BUT CUT WITH SOME TUPIAN BLOOD.

NOW UNACCUSTOMED TO WALKING ON TWO FEET, HE STAGGERS ALONG BEHIND THE BELLBOY TO HIS ROOM.

HE SPENDS THE NIGHT THRASHING ABOUT IN THE CONFINES OF A SINGLE BED.

...AS ERIS IN "THE MORGUE LITTÉRAIRE," AS AVOIR DU POIS IN "PUNIC LOVE," AS SALLY FAVUS IN "DEAF OR DUMB," AS SIS IN "THE LADY'S LOOPHOLE," AS MADAME HUZZA IN "THE LOMENT OF TRUTH," AS FANNY IN "SWAYBACK'S HOLLOW"...

ON THE AFTERNOON OF THE NEXT DAY, HE LEAVES THE HOTEL IN A STATE OF EXCITATION.

HE PASSES BELOW THE WINDOW OF AN ARTS CLUB WHERE A COUNTERFEIT EUROPEAN PAINTING IS ON DISPLAY,

RUNS ACROSS BROADWAY, FOLLOWING THE FAINT, YET IRRESISTIBLE, SCENT OF PICKLED HERRING

AND BY LUCK, FINDS HIMSELF AT THE STAGE DOOR OF THE NEW WORLD THEATER WHERE A DRESS REHEARSAL IS UNDERWAY.

FROM A SEAT IN THE FIRST BALCONY, HE SURVEYS THE ELABORATE STAGE DECORATION...

AS MY ANCESTORS FLED THE SPANISH INQUISITION, SO I NOW BID YOU A FOND FAREWELL!

AND TRIES TO FOLLOW THE ACTION OF THE PLAY.

DON'T BE A GRIND! COME WITH US FOR AN EVENING'S CAROUSAL ON MARKET STREET.

IF ALL THE WORLD'S A STAGE, I'D RATHER NOT FALL OFF IT.

WHEN MISS PATELLA MAKES HER ENTRANCE IN ACT 2, HE EMITS A STIFLED HOWL AND TEARS THE FEW CLOTHES FROM HIS BODY.

AH, I SEE, ANOTHER YOUNG SUPPLICANT AT THE ALTAR OF THESPIS. YES, PLEASE STEP THIS WAY.

IN ACT 2, SCENE 2, THE ACTOR MAYNARD DAIZY, IN THE ROLE OF MAJ. HAM, PUTS HIS ARM AROUND THE ACTRESS' WAIST IN AN EXAGGERATED SHOW OF AFFECTION.

YOUR HUSBAND MAY VOUCH FOR YOUR HISTRIONIC ABILITIES, BUT HE'S NO LONGER...

UNABLE TO DISTINGUISH BETWEEN THE ACTOR PLAYING NOAH AND THE REAL MAN, THE CREATURE THAT WAS ONCE MOISHE KETZELBOURD LEAPS TO THE STAGE

A PAYING CUSTOMER.

AND BITES INTO THE ACTOR'S SOFT ABDOMEN WITH THE COMBINED PASSION OF A HUNDRED-THOUSAND MILDLY TITILLATED SPECTATORS.

A QUICK-THINKING STAGEHAND PULLS A PISTOL AND SHOOTS AT WHAT HE TAKES TO BE A WOLF OR OVERGROWN JACKAL.

BANG!

FARVOUS!

DAIZY LIES SPRAWLED ACROSS A MINIATURE PERSPECTIVE OF BROADWAY, MORTALLY WOUNDED.

MAYNARD DAIZY IS CARRIED TO A NEARBY SURGEON'S OFFICE AND DECLARED DEAD.

THE NOSE AND CHIN ARE PUTTY.

THE ACTORS AND MANAGEMENT GATHER IN A TAVERN NEXT DOOR.

I'VE ARRANGED FOR A FUNERAL ON THURSDAY AND THEN ONE FULL DAY OF REHEARSAL WITH THE NEW MALE LEAD.

HERMAN WATTERBOTIL, A SHYLOCK SPECIALIST FROM PHILADELPHIA, IS ON HIS WAY HERE.

THE ANIMAL CARCASS IS UNCEREMONIOUSLY GATHERED INTO A BURLAP SACK AND PLACED WITH THE WEEK'S REFUSE IN AN ALLEY BEHIND THE THEATER.

STAGE

NEWS OF THE FREAK ATTACK SPREADS THROUGH THE CITY.

"IN ITS DEATH THROES, THE CREATURE EMITTED A STRANGE, DRAWN OUT CRY, MOST ACCURATELY REPRESENTED PHONETICALLY BY THE LETTERS: F-A-R-V-O-U-S."

FARVOUS?

A CURIOUS AMATEUR ZOOLOGIST STOPS BY TO HAVE A LOOK.

YOU SAY THE TAIL WAS DESTROYED BY THE FORCE OF THE PISTOL SHOT?

THE CARCASS WOULD HAVE BEEN REMOVED THE NEXT MORNING BY A PRIVATE CARTER OF WASTE HAD NOT MR. HIRAM BEEN APPRISED OF ITS WORTH.

IT IS A CREATURE UNLIKE ANY I HAVE SEEN BEFORE-DEFIES CLASSIFICATION! AS A PATRON OF THE NATURAL SCIENCES, IT BEHOOVES YOU TO BRING THIS DISCOVERY TO THE ATTENTION OF THE PUBLIC.

MAKE IT FIFTY DOLLARS EVEN AND WE HAVE A DEAL.

AND SO, WITH THE HELP OF TWO STRONG BOYS, THIS CURIOUS SPECIMEN IS PRESERVED FOR POSTERITY.

CAREFUL, CAREFUL, IT'S ALREADY MISSING A TAIL.

WITHIN THE WEEK, IT IS STUFFED, MOUNTED AND PUT ON DISPLAY IN THE MUSEUM'S FRONT ROOM.

THE TAIL IS A RECONSTRUCTION OF WHAT WE IMAGINE WAS ONCE THERE.

TICKET

A MAN IN AN INDIA RUBBER SUIT ENTERS THE SYNAGOGUE SHEARITH BATSAL.

HE QUESTIONS AN AGED MEMBER OF THE CONGREGATION,

NO, THIS IS SOMETHING NEW. HE WAS BORN HERE ON QUEEN STREET. I BOUGHT MEAT FROM HIS FATHER, ABRAHAM KISHON. THE FATHER DIED YOUNG IN AN INFLUENZA EPIDEMIC, NUSIN TOOK OVER THE BUSINESS AND MARRIED AN IDA WESTIL. THE POOR GIRL WAS KILLED BY A FALLING TREE. NATHAN BECAME CARELESS IN HIS WORK, HAD SOME TROUBLE INVOLVING A BEEF TONGUE AND THEN, I BELIEVE, FOLLOWED MORDECAI NOAH TO GRAND ISLAND.

AND THEN APPROACHES NATHAN KISHON.

SHOLEM-ALEYKHEM! GUT MORGN! ALABADO SEA SUI NUMBRE POR QUE SIEMPRE BIEN NOS DIO. HOW DO YOU DO.

I AM VERVEL KUNZO. I'VE TRAVELED HERE FROM BERLIN, UNDER THE UNOFFICIAL AUSPICES OF THE VEREIN FUR KULTUR UND WISSENSCHAFT DER JUDEN — THE SOCIETY FOR CULTURE AND SCIENCE OF THE JEWS — TO COMPILE A REPORT ON CULTURAL MANIFESTATIONS UNIQUE TO THE JEWS OF NEW YORK CITY. I COULDN'T HELP BUT NOTICE YOUR GRECO-ROMAN STYLE OF ATTIRE.

THIS IS A BED SHEET.

ARE THERE OTHER JEWS HERE IN THE CITY OF NEW YORK WHO DRESS IN THIS FASHION?

ARE ALL THE ENLIGHTENED JEWS OF BERLIN WEARING RUBBER SUITS THESE DAYS?

HA, HA, HA! NO, I TAKE AQUATIC STROLLS FOR EXERCISE, BUT ONE SHOULD TAKE NOTHING ON ITS FACE VALUE. THE JEW IS NOT A MUSEUM SPECIMEN TO BE ADMIRED ON SUNDAY AFTERNOONS.

LIKE ALL SOCIAL BEINGS, HE IS SUBJECT TO CONSTANT CHANGE AND DEVELOPMENT — A CREATURE OF HIS SURROUNDINGS. IT IS THIS SUBTLE, ONGOING METAMORPHOSIS THAT WE ENDEAVOR TO STUDY THROUGH THE RIGOROUS METHODS OF SCIENCE.

BUT TELL ME, HAVE YOU SLEPT OUT-OF-DOORS SINCE BIRTH? WERE BOTH YOUR PARENTS JEWS? HOW MANY JEWS ARE INVOLVED IN THE BEAVER TRADE? WHEN DID YOU CEASE PRACTICING KOSHER SLAUGHTER?

BUT ONE MORE QUESTION, IF I MAY? YOUR NASCENT PARTNERSHIP WITH THE LATE MR. ABEL MARAH, OF 27 WILLIAM STREET, TOUCHES UPON A SUBJECT OF GREAT INTEREST TO MYSELF AND OTHER CULTURAL SCIENTISTS.

BEAVER PELTS?

NO, BUT A KIND OF SKIN, YOU MIGHT SAY. APPARENTLY YOU ARE UNAWARE OF THE HISTORY OF THE GARMENT COMMONLY REFERRED TO AS A "FLESHING."

YOU SEE, THE ILLUSION OF AN UNDRAPED FIGURE IS TODAY EASILY ACHIEVED ON STAGE BY MEANS OF THE "FLESHING"—THE BODY IS CLOTHED FROM NECK TO FOOT IN A GOSSAMER, FLESH-COLORED GARMENT OF SILK: PART STOCKING, PART BREECHES, PART UNDER-VEST. BUT THIS WAS NOT ALWAYS SO!

WHEN WILLIAM LEE INVENTED THE STOCKING FRAME IN 1589, HE COULD NOT HAVE ENVISIONED THE THEATER OF TODAY WITH ITS PARTICULAR AND EXACTING DEMANDS FOR THE EFFECT OF UNVEILED FLESH. THIS DEVELOPMENT, COUPLED WITH ADVANCES IN EUROPEAN SILKWORM CULTURE, LED TO THE GARMENT OF WHICH I SPEAK.

BUT WHAT BROUGHT THE CURIOUS MOB TO THE THEATER IN THE FIRST PLACE WAS THE WONDROUS SPECTACLE OFFERED ON STAGE. AND THIS SPECTACLE DEPENDED, IN PART, FOR ITS SUCCESS UPON THE PERFECTED MANUFACTURE OF "FLESHINGS."

THE FOOTLIGHTS OF THE POPULAR THEATER CAST A RAKING BEAM OF INTELLECTUAL INQUIRY ACROSS ALL STRATA OF SOCIETY. THOSE IN THE PIT WERE NO LESS HARSHLY SCRUTINIZED THAN THOSE IN THEIR PRIVATE BOXES.

THE SOBER

WHAT SORT OF ATTRACTIONS DO YOU THINK LURED OUR CORELIGIONISTS OUT OF THE GHETTO AND INTO THE MAINSTREAM OF EUROPEAN CULTURE? WAS IT THE WIT OF MOLIÈRE, OR THE INGENIOUS STAGE MECHANISMS OF PIXÉRÉCOURT?

OR WAS IT SIMPLY THE OPPORTUNITY TO CAST AN EYE, WITHOUT SHAME, UPON THE LIVING, UNCLAD HUMAN FORM?

THE "FLESHING" ALLOWS US TO STUDY THE HUMAN FORM DIVINE, AS IT PASSES THROUGH A VARIETY OF DRAMATIC SITUATIONS, WITHOUT VIOLATING THE PRIVACY OR MODESTY OF THE INDIVIDUAL ACTOR.

THESE MONUMENTAL STRIDES IN "FLESHING" MANUFACTURE TOOK PLACE OVER SEVERAL GENERATIONS IN SMALL, ISOLATED WORKSHOPS IN BRUSSELS, PARIS AND MOULON. THE INVENTIVE NAME OF THE INVENTIVE GENIUSES RESPONSIBLE MAY HAVE BEEN RECORDED, BUT ARE NOW LOST.

IN 1820, FORTY YEARS AFTER THE DEATH OF VOLTAIRE, THE NAME OF ONE FAMILY OF JEWISH SILK MERCHANTS WAS LINKED WITH THESE INTERESTING GARMENTS.

THE SOLE IMPORTER OF "FLESHINGS" IN NEW YORK CITY IS A MR. CHARLES LORGNETTE. ACCORDING TO AN ADVERTISEMENT PLACED IN LAST TUESDAY'S EDITION OF "THE NATIONAL DISSEMBLER," THESE GARMENTS WERE BEING OFFERED FOR SALE TO THE GENERAL PUBLIC AT 27 WILLIAM STREET BY YOUR LATE PARTNER, MR. ABEL MARAH.

AND SO, BY ASSOCIATION, YOUR NAME BECOMES PART OF THIS INTRIGUING, AND NOW UNQUESTIONABLY JEWISH, CULTURAL HISTORY OF AMERICA.

AT THAT MOMENT, RABBI LOPEZ ARRIVES WITH TWO MEMBERS OF THE SHEARITH BATSAL BURIAL SOCIETY.

"MAY GOD COMFORT YOU AMONG ALL THOSE WHO MOURN FOR ZION AND JERUSALEM."

OUR CONDOLENCES ON THE DEATH OF YOUR FRIEND AND PARTNER, ABEL MARAH.

FREE TICKETS TO HIRAM'S MUSEUM?

AT THE WIFE'S REQUEST, THE BODY WILL BE RETURNED TO NEW YORK CITY FOR BURIAL. THE PERIOD OF MOURNING CAN BE CALCULATED FROM TONIGHT. WHEN THE BODY ARRIVES, IT WILL BE INTERRED AS QUICKLY AS POSSIBLE, AND THEN THE IMMEDIATE FAMILY CAN, IF THEY CHOOSE TO, SIT SHIVA FOR SEVEN DAYS.

HERE, DON'T BE SHY, TAKE TWO TICKETS FOR THE CURRENT EXHIBITION AT HIRAM'S MUSEUM —GRATIS!

IT MAY TAKE WEEKS FOR THE BODY TO ARRIVE. TO POSTPONE THE NATURAL EXPRESSION OF GRIEF FOR SO LONG SEEMS INHUMANE.

IDEALLY, THE BLOOD-STAINED BEDDING SHOULD ALSO BE RETRIEVED.

TAKE TWO, TAKE FOUR, TAKE AS MANY AS YOU LIKE! ALL I WANT IS TO PASS A FAVOR ALONG

MR. ZERUIAH, DON'T YOU SEE THAT WE'RE MAKING FUNERAL ARRANGEMENTS AMONGST BEREAVED PARTIES?

NOT INTERESTED? NO HARM DONE IN ASKING.

AS A PARTNER OF THE DECEASED, YOU WOULD NORMALLY REFRAIN FROM CONDUCTING BUSINESS FOR SEVEN DAYS.

AH, MRS. MARAH.

FREE TICKETS TO HIRAM'S MUSEUM!

YOUR HUSBAND AND I WERE, HOWEVER BRIEFLY, BUSINESS PARTNERS. AS IT WAS ON A BUSINESS TRIP THAT THIS TRAGEDY OCCURRED, THE COST OF THE FUNERAL, THE BURIAL AND ANY OTHER INCIDENTAL EXPENSES SHOULD BE CONSIDERED AN OPERATING EXPENSE OF THE BUSINESS, TO BE PAID FOR BY MYSELF, THE SOLE SURVIVING PARTNER.

AS PARTIAL PAYMENT FOR WINDOW GLAZING I WAS GIVEN FIFTY TICKETS. IT'S A FASCINATING EXHIBITION, BUT HOW MANY TIMES CAN I SEE IT?

YES, MR. ZERUIAH, THANK YOU. ON SECOND THOUGHT, I WILL TAKE TWO TICKETS.

TWO, FULL-PRICE ADULT ADMISSIONS, GOOD ANY DAY OF THE WEEK, YOURS ABSOLUTELY FREE WITH MY BEST WISHES

NATHAN, WILL YOU JOIN ME TOMORROW MORNING AT HIRAM'S MUSEUM? HOW CAN WE REFUSE AN OPPORTUNITY THRUST UPON US WITH SUCH INSISTENCE?

HIRAM'S MUSEUM ON BROADWAY?

YES, CORNER WORTH STREET, AND FOR TOMORROW, PLEASE, TROUSERS AND A SHIRT OUT OF RESPECT FOR THE OTHER MUSEUM PATRONS.

THE NEXT MORNING, RABBI LOPEZ AND NATHAN KISHON JOIN THE THRONG OUTSIDE OF HIRAM'S MUSEUM.

THIS WAY FOR "THE BOWERY BEHEMAH."

REMEMBER NATHAN, EVEN THESE SCIENTIFIC DISCOVERIES MUST BE TAKEN WITH A GRAIN OF SALT.

THE WELL-KNOWN THEATRICAL MANAGERS PEPSIN AND SHADRACH FILE PAST, AS THOUGH BEFORE AN OPEN CASKET.

AND TO THINK THAT POOR DAIZY LIVED ALL THOSE YEARS IN MORTAL FEAR OF THE CRITIC HORACE HEWALL.

TWO MEN DISCUSS THE COMPLEXITY OF MOUNTING SUCH A SPECIMEN.

SOON AFTER DEATH, A DELICATE HIDE SUCH AS THAT BECOMES DESICCATED LIKE OLD PARCHMENT—THERE'S NOTHING TO WORK WITH.

ONE YOUNG WAG PRETENDS TO RECOGNIZE HIS EMPLOYER.

AH, MR. TISHNELL, FANCY MEETING YOU HERE DURING BUSINESS HOURS!

THEY DIDN'T SAY IT WAS STUFFED.

A LECTURE, ON THE HALF HOUR, EXPLAINS THE CREATURE'S PLACE IN THE ANIMAL KINGDOM.

REST ASSURED, THIS IS NO BOGEYMAN OR MYTHOLOGICAL BEAST, IT IS SIMPLY ONE OF GOD'S CREATURES THAT WE HAVE NOT YET HAD THE PLEASURE TO ENCOUNTER. DR. HIRAM TELLS ME THAT IN PARTS OF SOUTH AMERICA THEY ARE COMMON—SOME HAVE EVEN BEEN DOMESTICATED AND TAUGHT TO CARRY PAPER MONEY IN THEIR MOUTH

TWO LEARNED MEN ARE FASCINATED BY THE CREATURE'S ORGANS OF REPRODUCTION.

YES, THE FORESKIN IS MISSING.

ACCORDING TO LEGEND, JACOB WAS BORN CIRCUMCISED—A SIGN OF DIVINE DESTINY.

AT THE URGING OF TWO UNIFORMED ATTENDANTS, THE LINE OF CURIOSITY SEEKERS MOVES ALONG AT A BRISK PACE.

PLEASE DON'T LINGER BEFORE THE BEAST, GIVE OTHERS A CHANCE!

YOUR ADVERTISEMENTS LED ME TO BELIEVE THAT IT WAS A LIVE ANIMAL.

YES, IT WAS ONCE LIVE, BUT IN THAT STATE WOULD NOT CONSENT TO PUBLIC DISPLAY.

OLD FRIENDS AND ACQUAINTANCES FROM ALL ECHELONS OF NEW YORK SOCIETY MINGLE IN A JOYOUS ATMOSPHERE OF SCIENTIFIC REVELATION.

HAD THIS CREATURE BEEN IDENTIFIED EARLIER, THE TRAGEDY MIGHT HAVE BEEN AVERTED.

THROUGH KNOWLEDGE, WE HAVE NOW ONE LESS THING TO FEAR. "I COUNT RELIGION BUT A CHILDISH TOY, AND HOLD THERE IS NO SIN BUT IGNORANCE."

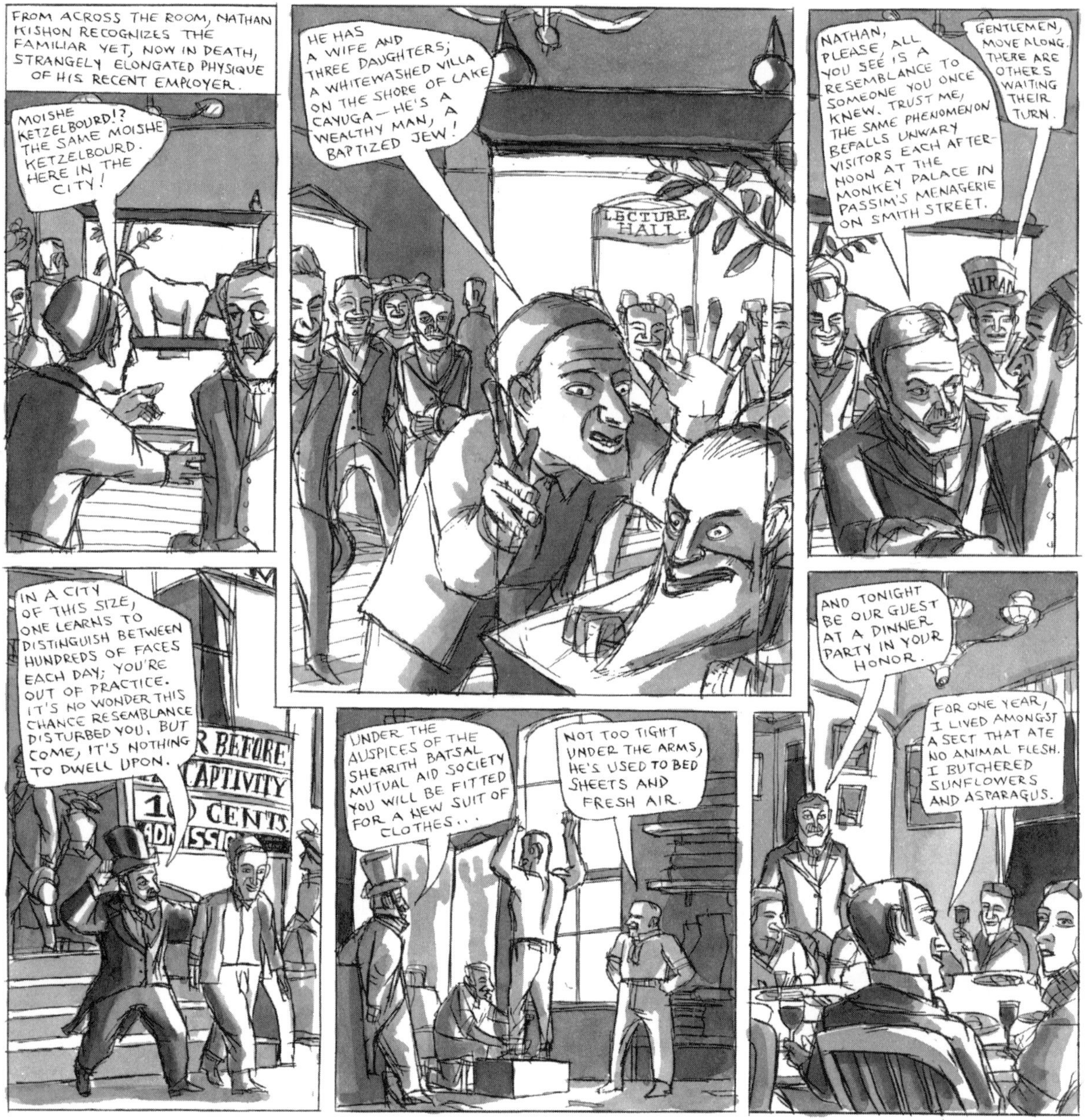
FROM ACROSS THE ROOM, NATHAN KISHON RECOGNIZES THE FAMILIAR YET, NOW IN DEATH, STRANGELY ELONGATED PHYSIQUE OF HIS RECENT EMPLOYER.
MOISHE KETZELBOURD!? THE SAME MOISHE KETZELBOURD. HERE IN THE CITY!
HE HAS A WIFE AND THREE DAUGHTERS; A WHITEWASHED VILLA ON THE SHORE OF LAKE CAYUGA—HE'S A WEALTHY MAN, A BAPTIZED JEW!
LECTURE HALL
NATHAN, PLEASE, ALL YOU SEE IS A RESEMBLANCE TO SOMEONE YOU ONCE KNEW. TRUST ME, THE SAME PHENOMENON BEFALLS UNWARY VISITORS EACH AFTERNOON AT THE MONKEY PALACE IN PASSIM'S MENAGERIE ON SMITH STREET.
GENTLEMEN, MOVE ALONG. THERE ARE OTHERS WAITING THEIR TURN.
IN A CITY OF THIS SIZE, ONE LEARNS TO DISTINGUISH BETWEEN HUNDREDS OF FACES EACH DAY; YOU'RE OUT OF PRACTICE. IT'S NO WONDER THIS CHANCE RESEMBLANCE DISTURBED YOU. BUT COME, IT'S NOTHING TO DWELL UPON.
UNDER THE AUSPICES OF THE SHEARITH BATSAL MUTUAL AID SOCIETY YOU WILL BE FITTED FOR A NEW SUIT OF CLOTHES...
NOT TOO TIGHT UNDER THE ARMS, HE'S USED TO BED SHEETS AND FRESH AIR.
AND TONIGHT BE OUR GUEST AT A DINNER PARTY IN YOUR HONOR.
FOR ONE YEAR, I LIVED AMONGST A SECT THAT ATE NO ANIMAL FLESH. I BUTCHERED SUNFLOWERS AND ASPARAGUS.

TWO DAYS OUT OF NEW YORK HARBOR, A DECK HAND SPIES THE BUOYANT DEBRIS OF A SHIPWRECK.

IN ACCORDANCE WITH AN UNWRITTEN AGREEMENT AMONG THE SHIPPING COMPANIES OF AMERICA AND EUROPE, ANCHOR IS DROPPED AND THE AFTERNOON DEVOTED TO IDENTIFYING THE REMAINS.

GOOD MORNING, MR. MARAH. DID YOU SLEEP WELL?

WITHIN THE HOUR, A PIECE OF A CABIN DOOR IS HAULED ABOARD.

THE "PALAMABRON," A SHIP OUT OF THE SOOLOO ISLANDS NEAR BORNEO... THROW IT BACK AND WEIGH ANCHOR!

AND STILL, EACH DAY, ISAAC AZARAEL VISITS THE NORTH RIVER DOCKS HOPING TO HEAR SOME RUMOR OR REPORT CONCERNING THE FATE OF THE "PALAMABRON."

HE WATCHES A MAN IN A WATERPROOF INDIA RUBBER SUIT ENTER THE RIVER.

AN OLD SAILOR OFFERS A POSSIBLE EXPLANATION.

THE "PALAMABRON" IS BLOWN OFF ITS COURSE BY A SUMMER STORM... LANDS SOMEWHERE IN THE WEST INDIES... THERE'S NO MONEY FOR REPAIRS ...THE CREW RUNS OFF AND THE CAPTAIN MEETS A NATIVE GIRL...

A NATIVE GIRL?

YES, AND THAT WOULD BE THE END OF IT.

[91]

UPON ARRIVING IN LONDON, MR. MARAH LEASES A ROOM ABOVE A TRUNK MAKER'S SHOP OFF WHITECHAPEL ROAD.

AVADE, IKH KEN A BISL YIDISH.

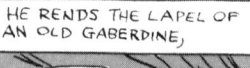

HE RENDS THE LAPEL OF AN OLD GABERDINE,

MY POOR WIFE AND FATHERLESS CHILD.

COVERS THE ROOM'S ONE MIRROR AND FOR SEVEN DAYS SITS ON A LOW STOOL.

THIS MOURNING BUSINESS SHOULDN'T BE OVERDONE.

AT THE END OF THE MONTH, HE CHANGES HIS CLOTHES AND SHAVES HIS FACE.

LIKE CASTOR AND POLLUX, I AM PERMITTED TO LIVE IN THIS WORLD, BUT MUST RETURN EVERY OTHER DAY TO THE LAND OF THE DEAD — A SAD, BUT NECESSARY COMPROMISE WITH THE REGISTRAR OF THE PUBLIC RECORD OFFICE.

I EFFECT MY OWN RESURRECTION EVERY OTHER DAY. UNDER THE ASSUMED NAME OF LUDWIG HULLAR, I VISIT MY BANKER'S OFFICE AND LOOK AFTER THE HEALTH OF MY INVESTMENTS.

SILK FUTURES UP 3%.

THEN I RETURN FOR A DAY TO THE TOMB OF A DEAD JEW FROM NEW YORK.

THE STREETS OF LONDON ARE FILLED WITH RUNAWAYS, WIFE DESERTERS AND LEGALLY DEAD MEN. IT'S A WAY OF LIFE OVER HERE.

"AN INSANE MAN FELL OVERBOARD YESTERDAY FROM THE STEAMBOAT 'NAHUM,' AND BUT FOR THE PROMPT ASSISTANCE OF THE SECOND CAPTAIN MUST HAVE PERISHED. WHEN RECOVERING FROM THE EFFECT OF HIS IMMERSION, HE ENQUIRED IF HE WAS REALLY DROWNED, OR ALIVE AS USUAL."

THE SOUNDS OF A VIOLENT COMMOTION EMANATE FROM ENOCH LETUSHIM'S ROOM ON THE SECOND FLOOR OF THE AMERICAN HOTEL.

IF THE CARBONATION OF LAKE ERIE PROVES TO BE COMMERCIALLY UNFEASIBLE, I MUST BE ABLE TO WASH MY HANDS OF IT AND DIRECT MY ENERGIES IN ANOTHER, MORE FRUITFUL, DIRECTION!

21

AY! AY!

THE GOVERNMENT HAS LEGISLATED THAT IT SHOULD BE SO! THE CORPORATION IS AN IMMORTAL ENTITY BROUGHT FORTH FOR THE BENEFIT OF THE PUBLIC. THE CORPORATION'S DIRECTOR, HOWEVER, IS A MERE MORTAL, CAPABLE OF MISCALCULATIONS AND LAPSES OF JUDGEMENT.

I AM MR. CORYZA, THE MANAGER OF THIS HOTEL!

21 WAH!

BANKRUPTCY IS THE LEGAL RECOGNITION OF THAT SIMPLE FACT; A MEANS OF PRESERVING THAT RARE HUMAN QUALITY: THE ENTREPRENEURIAL SPIRIT!

OY, RAKH-MONES!

WHO ELSE WOULD HAVE THOUGHT OF SUCH A GRANDIOSE SCHEME? UNTIL NOW, MEN WERE CONTENT TO DRINK WATER CARBONATED IN THE LOCAL CELLAR TANKS OF DIS-REPUTABLE BREWERIES AND CHEMICAL FACTORIES.

WAH! WAH!

AMERICAN HOTEL

IN THE HOTEL'S FIRST-FLOOR DINNING ROOM A LUNCHEON BANQUET IS DISRUPTED.

I SAW A BETTER WAY! THAT THE MECHANICAL SKILL REQUIRED TO REALIZE MY PLAN DOES NOT YET EXIST — THAT THE CAPITAL NEEDED IS NOT FORTHCOMING — SHOULD NOT BE LAID UPON MY HEAD!

AYCH! AYCH!

GOOD LUCK

THE MANAGER OPENS THE DOOR WITH A SKELETON KEY

AND YET THE PUBLIC IS POISED TO DISGRACE ME; TO LAUGH AT MY LOSSES, MOCK AT MY GAINS — AND WHAT IS THEIR REASON? DO I NOT SUFFER THE HEAT OF AUGUST THE SAME AS THEY DO? AM I NOT CHAINED TO THE SAME DUNGEON WALL AS THEY ARE — A PRISONER OF HISTORICAL CIRCUMSTANCE?

FAOUK! FAOUK!

TO FIND A REGISTERED GUEST ON THE FLOOR IN A BATTERED CONDITION.

YOUR SUPPLY OF DIRT IS APPARENTLY INEXHAUSTIBLE, BUT MY ENERGIES ARE OF A FINITE QUANTITY.

NOTHING, NOTHING, A BUSINESS DISPUTE. CALL THE DOCTOR.

IN THE EXCITEMENT FOLLOWING A DRESS REHEARSAL OF "THE JEW OF NEW YORK,"

SIGNORE BATTELLO, OR HIS ASSISTANT, FORGETS TO EXTINGUISH THE FIRE UNDER THE "PICKLED HERRING AROMA" APPARATUS.

THE ACTORS GO TO A NEARBY TAVERN FOR DRINKS.

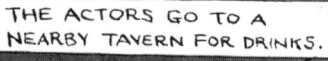

THE MANAGERS, PEPSIN AND SHADRACH, MEET AN INFLUENTIAL JOURNALIST FOR DINNER.

YES, YES… A FINE MADEIRA.

THE PLAY'S AUTHOR, PROF. SOLIDUS, RETURNS TO HIS ROOM ON THE THEATER'S THIRD FLOOR,

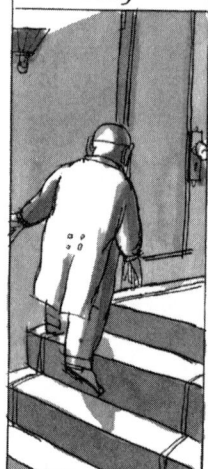

WITHIN MINUTES, HE AND HIS LITERARY WORKS ARE CONSUMED BY A RAGING FIRE.

SNIFF SNIFF SOMETHING BURNING IN THE KITCHEN?

DEVOURS A TIN OF BISCUITS AND THREE DRIED SAUSAGES

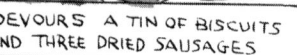

AND THEN FALLS ASLEEP.

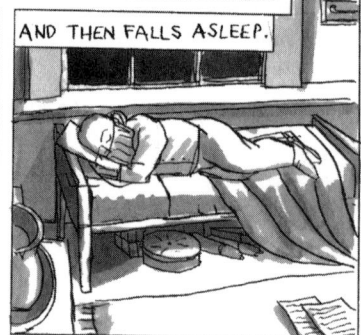

A NIGHT WATCHMAN SOUNDS AN ALARM WHICH IS RELAYED, IN TURN, TO THE MESNOMER BELL TOWER

BUNG HONG BUNG

HUSKY YOUNG MEN LEAVE OFF IN THE MIDST OF EATING AND FORNICATING

TO DON THEIR RED FLANNEL SHIRTS AND LEATHER HATS, AND JOIN THEIR FELLOW VOLUNTEERS IN A ROUSING NIGHT OF FIRE FIGHTING.

THE FLOTILLIAN BRIGADE NO. 7 AND THE "VEAL CHOPS" OF ENGINE COMPANY 4 BOTH SET OUT AT BREAKNECK SPEED IN A VAINGLORIOUS ATTEMPT TO BE FIRST ON THE SCENE.

THE TWO COMPANIES MEET HEAD-ON TO VIE, IN GOOD-NATURED RIVALRY, FOR A SUPERIOR PUMPING POSITION IN RELATION TO THE BURNING EDIFICE.

NEW WORLD THEATER

MEANWHILE, THE MEMBERS OF THE 15th HYDRANT COMPANY FIGHT AMONGST THEMSELVES FOR THE HONOR OF PULLING THE PLUG.

SOMEONE SUGGESTS TAPING INTO THE LAKE ERIE SODA WATER COMPANY'S FOUNTAIN ACROSS THE STREET.

AN INEXHAUSTIBLE SUPPLY OF WATER RIGHT HERE, AT HAND!

LAKE ERIE SODA WATER

A SINGLE ARC OF CARBONATED WATER RISES AND FALLS IN THE NIGHT AIR.

HOLD OFF BOYS, THE HOSE HAS FALLEN LIMP!

THE PIPE IS TRACED TO THE BUILDING'S CELLAR, WHERE A SHORT LENGTH OF COPPER TUBING ENTERS A NOW-EMPTY WOODEN CASK.

"PROPERTY OF THE MASTODON SODA WATER COMPANY, MULBERRY STREET, NEW YORK CITY."

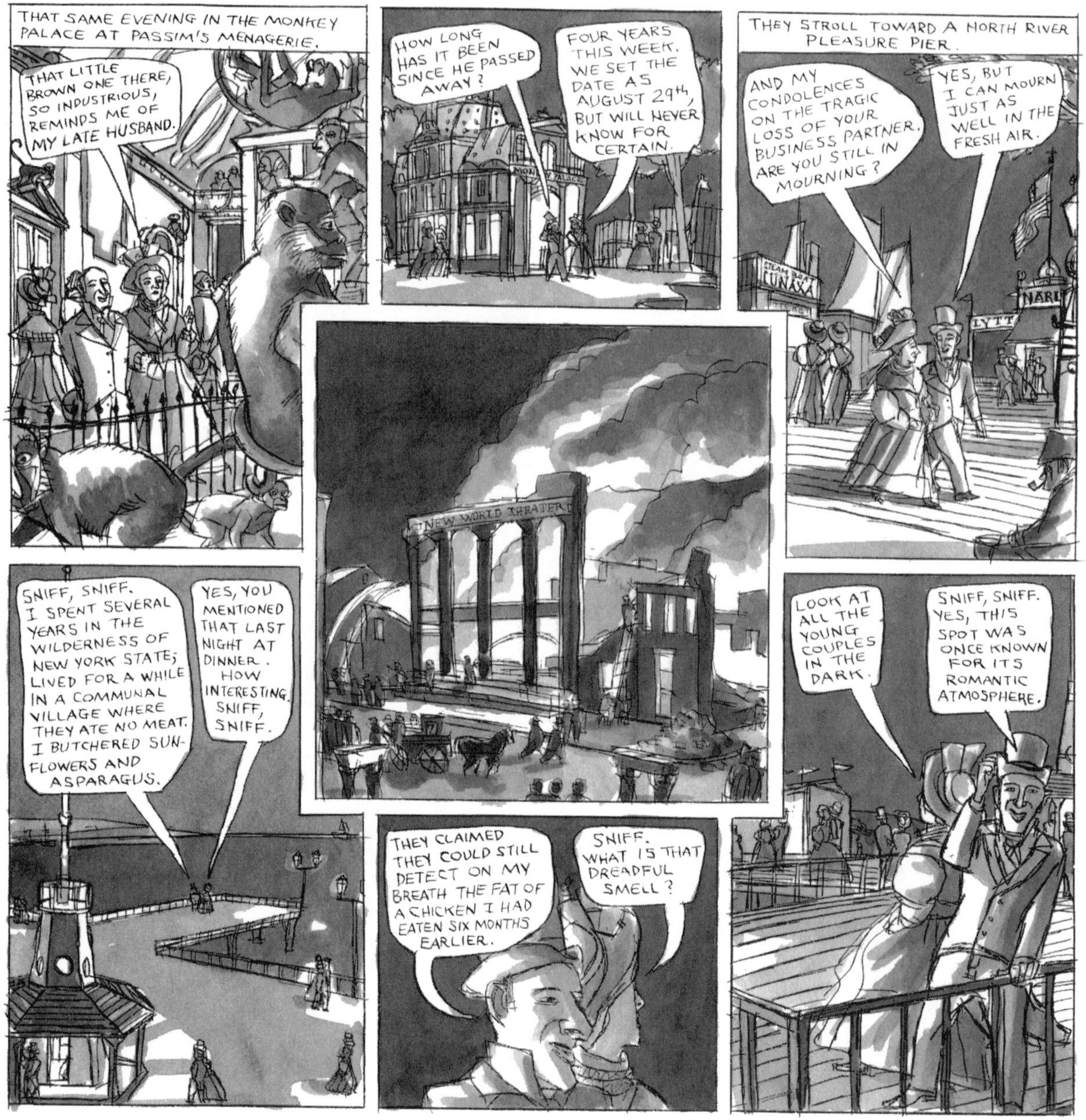
THAT SAME EVENING IN THE MONKEY PALACE AT PASSIM'S MENAGERIE.
THAT LITTLE BROWN ONE THERE, SO INDUSTRIOUS, REMINDS ME OF MY LATE HUSBAND.
HOW LONG HAS IT BEEN SINCE HE PASSED AWAY?
FOUR YEARS THIS WEEK. WE SET THE DATE AS AUGUST 29th, BUT WILL NEVER KNOW FOR CERTAIN.
MONKEY PALACE
THEY STROLL TOWARD A NORTH RIVER PLEASURE PIER.
AND MY CONDOLENCES ON THE TRAGIC LOSS OF YOUR BUSINESS PARTNER. ARE YOU STILL IN MOURNING?
YES, BUT I CAN MOURN JUST AS WELL IN THE FRESH AIR.
NEW WORLD THEATER
SNIFF, SNIFF. I SPENT SEVERAL YEARS IN THE WILDERNESS OF NEW YORK STATE; LIVED FOR A WHILE IN A COMMUNAL VILLAGE WHERE THEY ATE NO MEAT. I BUTCHERED SUNFLOWERS AND ASPARAGUS.
YES, YOU MENTIONED THAT LAST NIGHT AT DINNER. HOW INTERESTING. SNIFF, SNIFF.
THEY CLAIMED THEY COULD STILL DETECT ON MY BREATH THE FAT OF A CHICKEN I HAD EATEN SIX MONTHS EARLIER.
SNIFF. WHAT IS THAT DREADFUL SMELL?
LOOK AT ALL THE YOUNG COUPLES IN THE DARK.
SNIFF, SNIFF. YES, THIS SPOT WAS ONCE KNOWN FOR ITS ROMANTIC ATMOSPHERE.

A MAN IN A WATERPROOF INDIA RUBBER SUIT WANDERS ALONG THE BANK OF THE NORTH RIVER

"THE EARLY SPANISH WRITERS UNANIMOUSLY RECOGNIZED AND ACKNOWLEDGED THE MANIFOLD ANALOGIES WHICH DEMONSTRATE THE TRANSFERENCE OF THE LEVITICAL ECONOMY TO THE NEW CONTINENT.

READING TO HIMSELF FROM A DAMP OLD PAMPHLET.[1]

BUT WHILE SOME OF THEM DISCERNED IN THIS CIRCUMSTANCE AN INDISPUTABLE PROOF OF THE HEBREW ORIGIN OF THE NEWLY DISCOVERED PEOPLE,

OTHERS ACCOUNTED FOR THIS ALMOST FAC SIMILE RESEMBLANCE BY ASSERTING THAT SATAN HAD COUNTERFEITED IN THE PEOPLE (WHOM HE HAD CHOSEN FOR HIMSELF)

THE HISTORY, MANNERS, CUSTOMS, TRADITIONS, AND EXPECTATIONS OF THE HEBREWS

IN ORDER THAT THEIR MINDS MIGHT THUS BE RENDERED INACCESSIBLE

TO THE FAITH WHICH HE FORESAW THE CHURCH WOULD IN DUE TIME INTRODUCE AMONGST THEM."

THE END

[1] "The Ten Tribes of Israel Historically Identified with the Aborigines of the Western Hemisphere" by Mrs. Simon

.hat can ...

for sure.

𝕻ortraits of 𝕰minent 𝕸en

BEN KATCHOR,

THE author of this book lives in New York City. He is well known for his weekly comic-strip work published under the titles "Julius Knipl, Real Estate Photographer," and "The Cardboard Valise." These strips appear in the *Forward* and a dozen other newspapers around the country. He also produces a monthly comic-strip for the magazine *Metropolis*.

LEFT-OVER FROM DINNER

After a heavy meal, one is not dispos⸱
⸱aking on heavy mental labo⸱

THE LAKE ERIE SODA-WATER COMPANY.

A Cross-sectional View Showing the Wastage of Soda-Water on a Representative City Street.

AN INQUIRY INTO PROFLIGATE BEHAVIOR.

At this time in history, the population of The City of New York is close to 1,000,000 souls—each consuming an average of six glasses of soda-water each day, or 375,000 gal. of liquid. The amount of carbonated waters drawn each day from the Canadian shore of Lake Erie is approximately 100,000,000 gal. Careful investigation has revealed that 96,250,000 gal. of this precious commodity are wasted each day.

How can the rational mind explain this prodigious loss of liquid wealth? By what mechanism of abuse does the average soda-water drinker discard a quantity of beverage equal to that which he consumes?

Subscribers who are not on the meter system have been known to let their tap "run" until the soda-water reaches the temperature of a chilled drink. They have no regard for the fact that thousands of dollars in capital improvements to the entire system are worn-down by heedless "running" of their tap.

If the present wastage of soda-water is not curtailed, through educational or compulsory means, the Great Lake Erie will be drained dry in the next hundred years.

Furthermore, the supply of this exquisite beverage is maintained at the expense of a privately held corporation. For how long can The Lake Erie Soda-Water Company absorb these crippling losses? What is the future of carbonated water in our great metropolis? Can the Federal government be called upon to underwrite the pleasures of a few well-to-do New Yorkers?

pl. 1

SALTED PEANUTS

pl. 2

pl. 3

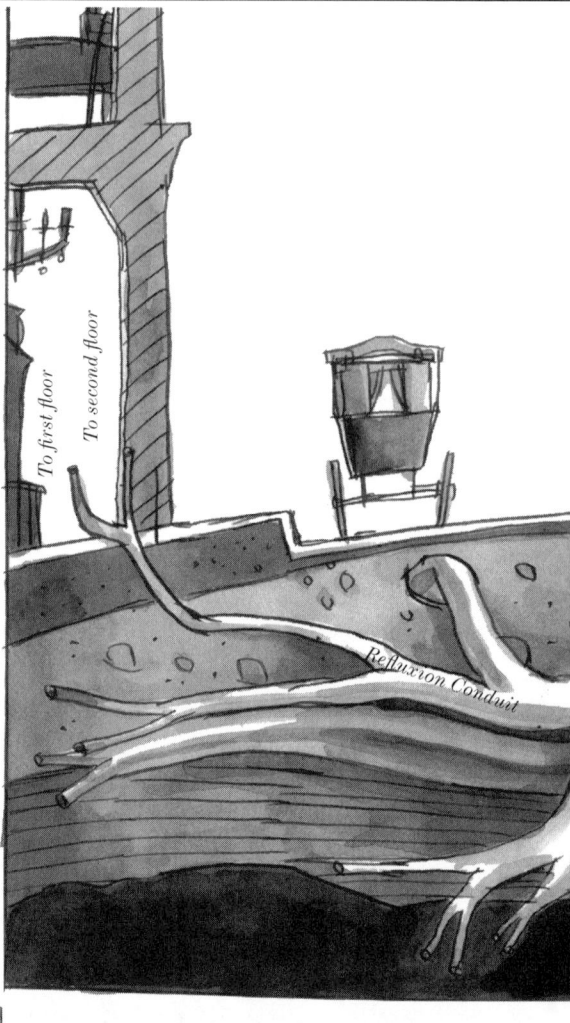

To first floor

To second floor

Refluxion Conduit

L. Erie

Lake Erie is 260 miles long and, on average, 40 miles wide. Although Erie is the most southerly of the Great Lakes, it is the most susceptible to freezing in winter. This is due to the general shallowness of its waters, the greatest depth being no more than 15 to 20 fathoms. The Canadian side is composed of majestic clay banks which naturally lend themselves to man-made carbonation.

pl. 4